Blow Out the Moon

Blow Out the Moon

by Libby Koponen

Megan Tingley Books
LITTLE, BROWN AND COMPANY
New York ⸱⸱ Boston

Little, Brown and Company

Time Warner Book Group
1271 Avenue of the Americas, New York, NY 10020
Visit our Web site at www.lb-kids.com

First Edition

Library of Congress Cataloging-in-Publication Data

Koponen, Libby.
Blow out the moon / by Libby Koponen. — 1st ed.
p. cm.
"Megan Tingley books."
Summary: A fictionalized account of the author's childhood experiences
moving from the United States to London, England, and attending
a boarding school.
ISBN 0-316-61443-2
[1. Moving, Household — Fiction.   2. Boarding schools — Fiction.
3. Schools — Fiction.   4. England — Fiction.]   I. Title
PZ7.K836145B1 2004   2003054603
[Fic] — dc22

10   9   8   7   6   5   4   3   2   1

Q-FF

Printed in the United States of America

Acknowledgments

This book is based on a true story, but some of the real things had been lost by the time we were doing the pictures. So other people made substitutes: Alex White drew the ocean liner card; other children, whose parents wanted their names kept private, made fortune catchers and played cat's cradle and let the pictures be printed—and the author and publisher thank them. Marza's daughter gave us permission to use the pictures from later Sibton Park school catalogs: thank you, Barbara Service. Thanks also to Kevin R. Tam for the photographs of the *France* and the *Liberté*; BBC Wales *Capture Wales* and Daniel Meadows, photographer, for the Wellingtons; Jim Gaston for the pens; and Charles Owen & Company, headwear manufacturer, for the English riding hat. All used with permission. Special thanks to Miranda Hickox, who edited an early version of this story when she was nine and read it again and again after that.

When the author says something is real, it is. The dolls and their tea set, all the letters and stories and school compositions, the Sibton Park clothes list, and the quote from the catalog are real. So are the photographs she took of her friends at Sibton Park and the horse in the field. She took the picture of the window in

London later, but it's the same window. The author's father, Arthur Koponen, took the pictures of her reading, all the family photographs, and the paddock steps with Sibton Park in the background.

Some people may be curious about the illustrations from old books: they are real too. The artists were Arthur Rackham (*Peter Pan in Kensington Gardens*), Kay Nielsen ("East of the Sun and West of the Moon"), Edmund Evans from a design by "Phiz" ("Hansel and Gretel") and H. P. Thorpe (*Pride and Prejudice*).

The author thanks Megan Tingley for her perceptive comments and strong support, Christine Cuccio for good judgement and a major save, Billy Kelly for the beautiful fonts and layout, Renée Gelman, for making it such a beautiful book, and Alvina Ling, who believed in the book from the beginning and read it all over and over, without ever losing her enthusiasm or her temper. Thank you, Alvina.

To my mother, Sally Rumble Koponen, who always encouraged me to write and saved all my stories — even when we moved.

Blow Out the Moon

Chapter One: News

I'll start the story one fall afternoon, when I had been sent home from my friend Henry's house.

"I suppose you were the ringleader, Libby?" his mother had said. She usually said that when we got caught doing something; I thought of it as a compliment. It wasn't meant to be one, I know, but the word made me think of the circus.

Henry stuck up for me: He said he'd wanted to see how much noise we could make, too, and so had everyone else. I'm glad he said that. His mother probably would have sent everyone home anyway, not just me, but it was still a good thing to say.

The air was colder on the way home, and the sky was orange at the edges and pale in the middle. But there was still time to play outside before dinner, maybe enough time for other people to come over.

I ran the rest of the way. When I opened our door, my father was there, talking to my sister Emmy. He looked excited.

"I'm home early because it's a special occasion," he said, but he wouldn't say why, even when Emmy asked in a cute way.

"Daddy!" I said. (I never try to act cute.) "You shouldn't have said anything if you weren't going to tell us. It's not fair." But that just made him laugh more. "At least give us a hint."

"It's something that will be a big change for all of us — especially you and Emmy. No more questions. We're eating soon, and I'll tell you at the table."

When dinner was ready, Emmy turned out the lights and I lit the candles (Emmy and I take turns doing that), while our little brother and sister got in their places.

It WAS a special dinner: lasagna! We ate while our parents talked: we're not allowed to talk unless one of them asks us a question. This is a rule most families don't have, I know. We have it because my father says "adult conversation is very important." He says most people stop talking to each other when they're married, and he doesn't want that to happen to him and my mother.

So they, mostly my father, talk, and sometimes I listen and sometimes I don't; that night, I listened even to some of the really boring things, but I still didn't find out what the news was.

Emmy and Willy, who sit next to each other, were doing something on their laps — passing something back and forth, I think. I couldn't see what. Willy was giggling, though. Bubby played with her food. I wrote on the table. This is kind of a strange habit, I guess, but I like to do it. I hold my pointer finger between my thumb and my middle finger, as though my finger is a pencil, and then I write with it.

My father saw me doing it.

"It's too bad no one will ever read all the great novels Libby's written on the dining room table," he said. (He knows I want to be a writer when I grow up — everyone who knows me knows that!) Then he and my mother laughed.

I didn't. Emmy didn't laugh, either. We didn't make a face at each other — those kinds of faces count as talking — but we both hate it when he's sarcastic. Grown-ups are never funny when they say sarcastic things, and I wish they wouldn't do it, especially to children. Of course, I didn't say that. I wrote it on the table, though.

Finally, he said he would tell us the news.

"We're moving to England for six months. I've been transferred to the London office of J. Walter Thompson. They wanted me to go alone, and come back for a visit after three months, but I said, 'No, I want to bring my family with me.' So we're all going."

He said that he would go first, and my mother would bring us over on an ocean liner, and he'd find a place for us to live in London and a school for Emmy and me — and maybe Willy, too.

"English schools are different," he said. "It will be an interesting experience for you."

The Liberté's maiden voyage into New York. (You can see the New York skyline in the background.)

I was still trying to imagine an ocean liner.

"Will we be on the ship for a long time? Will it have a gangplank and portholes?" I said.

"Five nights. You'll sleep in cabins with portholes and bunk beds," he said (Emmy and I have always wanted bunk beds). "You and Emmy will be in one cabin, Mommy and Willy and Bubby in the one next door. It's a famous ocean liner called the *Liberté*."

"Like Libby!" I said.

"*Liberté* is French for 'liberty.' You'll have a wonderful time on the ship — there are all kinds of things for children to do."

He said that in a few years "that form of travel" wouldn't exist, and how he wanted us to "have the experience." He couldn't take the boat with us because there wasn't time, but on the way home, we'd all go on one together.

He talked about ocean liners for a long time: I pictured wind and ladies in long dresses going up the gangplank and the sound of a foghorn. Being on one did seem pretty exciting.

That night, when Emmy and I were having our bath, I tried to figure out how something that big, and made of metal, could float.

"I just don't understand why it doesn't sink," I said. I had brought a little iron horse of mine into the tub with us.

"Look — even this little horse goes straight to the bottom every time. And Daddy said the boat is bigger than Great Oak Lane."

I thought about it more in bed, while I was listening to the cars go by. I like falling asleep to those sounds: first the engine from far away getting closer and louder — it sounds lonely and adventurous from far away, then loud and exciting when the lights sweep the room. But no matter how much I thought about it, I still couldn't understand how a huge boat made out of metal could float.

And then I tried to imagine what it would be like to live in another *country*. I put my feet up on the wall at the head of the bed, and my hands behind my head, and thought. I couldn't picture it at all (except for London Bridge, which I imagined as arching over a river, with little towerlike houses on it). But even though I didn't know exactly what it would be like, it felt exciting — a *real* adventure, not a made-up one, that I'd be in myself.

Chapter Two:
Telling Henry

The first thing I thought of when I woke up was telling my friends: especially The Gang and Henry. The Gang is Peg and Pat (twins), Kenny, Emmy, and I. We've known each other almost all our lives, and we always walk to school together. We meet at Peg and Pat's.

That day was like fall and summer at the same time. The light was pale, there were dead leaves on the sidewalk, but my new school clothes felt itchy and hot by the time we got to Peg and Pat's (we ran).

As usual, Kenny was there first, waiting, and Peg and Pat weren't ready: Mrs. Tampone was still brushing Pat's hair. Pat's hair is long and shiny and black. It never looks messy — no matter what we do, it stays shining and in place. Even her part always stays straight! Pat's face always looks clean, too, even when we've been playing outside all day — not like ours. (I once heard my mother say, sighing, to another mother, "My children all have that pinky-white skin that looks dirty so quickly.")

Pat wriggled and made faces — her mother shook her head and smiled at me, probably because I was the only one watching.

"Do you do that when your mother brushes your hair?" she said.

My mother never brushes my hair. I do it myself; she's busy

with Willy and Bubby in the morning. But I didn't answer — it was none of Mrs. Tampone's business, anyway.

While Peg was brushing their dog's hair, Kenny kept trying to grab the brush, and Peg told Emmy to tickle him, and she did. Duke jumped up at Kenny, barking hysterically.

"Lib, help!" Kenny shouted (between laughs). "Two girls and a dog against me!"

"Neighborly love, neighborly love," Pat sang (she always sings this when two friends are fighting — when two sisters are fighting, she sings, "sisterly love, sisterly love").

Finally the twins were ready and we ran out and Mrs. Tampone closed the door and I could say, "Guess what? — Emmy, don't tell!"

"You're going to be allowed to play outside after dinner," Kenny said. All the other guesses were just as wrong and I didn't waste much time on that.

"We're moving to England for six months! Our whole family! And we're going over on an ocean liner called the *Liberté* — on one of the last voyages that ship will ever make."

"And we'll go to an English school where we might have to wear a uniform because all the English kids will wear one," Emmy said.

"Do you think they'll like you?" Pat said.

"Why wouldn't they?" I said.

"Maybe they'll say" (here, she kind of stuck her nose in the air and made a face), "'Uh, American girls!'"

"They'll probably like us," I said. "And if they don't, who cares? Come on — let's run!"

I wanted to tell Henry.

At the playground, we split up as usual (at school, we play with kids in our own classes). I looked around the playground for Henry: The paved part was full of little kids and girls. Two in my class were turning a long jump rope and shouting:

"All in toGETHER girls!

How do you like the WEATHer girls!

JANuary! FEBruary . . ."

while other girls jumped into the game.

I like some of the rhymes, but I don't play much jump rope. At school, I usually play with the boys. I ran to the back of the play-ground, where most of them were, and that's where Henry was — he gave me a huge wave. I waved back as hard as I could (I really, really like Henry) and ran over.

He was in the middle of a fast dodgeball game. When no one caught it, the ball hit the fence really hard: so hard that the old metal fence shook and squeaked. I watched until the ball came close enough, then jumped up and got it. I threw it to Henry and said, "Can I play?"

"Sure," Henry said (to me). And then to the others: "She can be on my team."

"Girls don't play dodgeball!" a boy I'd never seen before said.

"*She* does; she's good," Henry said.

I ran in next to him, and when that boy threw the ball straight at me, hard (it hurt my stomach), I caught it and held it and he was out. I threw low and hard, but I didn't get anyone else out until just before the bell rang and we had to go in. Henry and I walked together.

"I saw that last catch you made," he said, smiling.

"My family is moving to England," I said. "We're going on an ocean liner — for six months."

His smile went away fast and he didn't say anything at first. Then: "Six months," he said, frowning. "That means you'll be gone until almost the end of the year."

When he said that, it felt like we would be GONE. That sounds silly. (It IS silly: Of course, if we were going, we would be gone!) But it was still surprising: Before, I hadn't thought much about being gone, just about *going* — the adventure of it.

"That *is* a pretty long time," I said.

I thought about what it would be like to be away from him and everyone else (like The Gang!) while we walked into the school and up the stairs and to our desks — in opposite corners of the classroom.

They were in opposite corners because the teacher separated us at the very beginning of the year: She put him at the front left desk and me at the back right one. But we can still tell each other things. Once, when the teacher said everyone would have partners for a class trip, Henry turned around in his seat and eagerly stretched out his hand to me with a big smile. I knew that meant, "Will you be my partner?" and of course, I nodded.

I was thinking about that when the final bell rang. Miss Jessup stood up and looked at all of us. She has a puffy face like the kind of dog that has drooping flaps for cheeks and sad eyes. When everyone was looking at her, she said, "Good morning, class. I will now call the roll."

Just as she finished, I thought of something — and since she was already facing the flag, and we were pushing our chairs back to stand up, I could signal it to Henry right away, if he looked back at me. He did, but before I could act it out, we had to look serious for the Pledge of Allegiance.

It IS kind of serious, to me. I looked at the flag, put my right hand over my heart, and said:

> *I pledge allegiance*
> *to the flag*
> *of the United States of America.*
> *And to the Republic*
> *for which it stands,*
> *one nation*
> *under God,*
> *indivisible,*
> *with liberty and justice for all.*

Liberty! I like saying that. I wish Libby were short for "liberty" instead of Elizabeth. And it was a great name for a ship, too.

The morning went by even more slowly than usual: She passed out workbooks, snapping each one down as though it was a card she was dealing in an exciting hand, and while we worked, she watched us. She said, "Libby, I don't see you marking your paper."

Someone else wasn't doing his work, either — Miss Jessup said, "David, you won't find any answers staring out that window."

I looked out — the windows went all the way up to the ceiling, but there was nothing to see: just blank blue sky, and the blinds. The blinds were rolled up, flapping (they sounded like sails) in the same little wind that rustled the papers on Miss Jessup's desk and lifted some of the girls' hair.

At school, time goes by *so* slowly! I looked up at the clock: It's very old-fashioned. The numbers are Roman numerals, and the hands have pointed tips like valentine arrows. The minute hand doesn't move invisibly, as it does on most

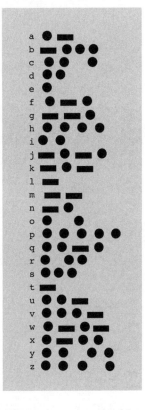

Morse code translates the alphabet into these dots and dashes, which you can send as long and short sounds or flashes of light. Henry and I used to tap it on our desks to each other, before the teacher moved us.

clocks — it stays still and then every few minutes jumps ahead (to the new time) with a low whirring sound.

It was only 10:10. I was waiting for the hand to jump to 10:12 or 10:13 (sometimes it jumps two minutes, sometimes three) when she told me again to get to work, so I did.

Finally it was lunchtime. We had to walk down the stairs, without talking (that's a rule); as soon as we got outside, we could run. I did — I was BURSTING with energy. I jumped down the steps and ran to the corner. Henry did, too. Then we had to wait for the policeman to cross us.

"I had an idea," I said. "We can write letters!"

I could tell he liked the idea (by the way his eyes changed) even before he said, "And we can use code for things that are really private!"

"You mean — make one up?" I said, walking backwards. "Or write the Morse code dots and dashes?"

"I was thinking — make one up."

"That would be more private," I said.

From across the street, a boy in our class yelled that I had told Miss Jessup on him. (Of course, I hadn't.) Before I could answer, Henry shouted, really angrily: "She did not! I've known her since she was in kindergarten and she doesn't snitch!"

Henry always sticks up for me.

We walked along, first scuffing, then kicking, the leaves up from the sidewalk.

"When are you leaving?" he said.

"In two weeks."

"Then you can come over on Saturday!"

"I'll ask," I said. "Oh, I hope I can! We could play pioneers!"

"And finish our fort!" Henry said.

Above me, the leaves blazed yellow, as though the sun was coming right through them. Then one leaf fell down kind of slowly, twirling in the sun.

I ran to catch it — and I did catch it. Henry saw me and we both started laughing (it wasn't funny, we were just happy). Then another leaf twirled down, slowly — it was yellow, too. We both ran for it, and I wished everything could stay just as it was at that moment forever and ever . . . that it could always be this sunny fall day and Henry and I could always be in it together.

Chapter Three: Two Tea Parties

But on Saturday I couldn't go to Henry's, because an English boy and his mother were coming over for tea. My mother set everything up on the living room table (including the fat silver sugar bowl filled with sugar lumps — you take them out with silver tongs), and reminded us to pass things to the guests first. One good thing about our mother is that she never corrects our manners in front of other people. I wish everyone's mother would do this. I hate it when parents say things like "What do you say?" or scold their children in front of you.

When the guests came, the mothers introduced themselves and said ladylike things like, "Please call me Sally."

Then Mrs. Grant said, "And this is my son Neil."

"And this is my oldest daughter, Libby." My mother squeezed my shoulders and I knew she wanted me to say hello politely, so I did. Emmy did, too; Willy and Bubby just stood behind my mother, but they did stop giggling. Then we all sat down and the mothers talked.

We looked at Neil and he looked at us. Everything about him was light. His hair was yellow-white — more white than yellow — and his skin was pink and white, even more than ours, and his eyes were light blue and the whites were very white. He had bangs, which most boys don't. Most boys I know have crew cuts.

Neil ate slowly and carefully, wiping his mouth after every bite. He sat up very straight — even his clothes were very straight — and he didn't spill anything, not even his tea. He seemed like a real goody-goody. You probably have already figured out that I'm not. But I haven't said what I look like yet, so I'll describe myself now, too. I'm short for my age — everyone in my class is taller than I am. But I'm strong. I can beat Kenny at wrestling and most of the boys in my class, too.

My hair is as straight as hair can be, and it's cut in a straight line across my forehead and straight along the sides. In pictures, my eyes look straight at the camera; they're blue. I am not the kind of child grown-ups ever call "cute" or "just darling."

Emmy can be that kind of child. She has curly blonde hair and she likes to be cuddled and to sit on grown-ups' laps.

The mothers talked — it was pretty boring, except when Mrs. Grant said, "What is peanut butter?" I'd never met a mother who didn't know that.

The cookies were gone, so I asked if I could be excused, and she said Emmy and I could take Neil upstairs. That really meant that we could only go if we brought him with us.

Neil was taller than I was, too; but I bet I was stronger. On the way up, I said, "It's lucky that you or your mother didn't pour the tea."

"Why?"

"Because you're English and we're American. If you'd given me a cup of tea, I'd have had to dump it out — in honor of the Boston Tea Party."

I was about to tell him what the Boston Tea Party was when he said, "Rubbish."

I was too surprised to say anything. Then he said, "My mother has given tea to lots of Americans before and THEY never poured it on the floor."

"Well, maybe other people don't do it, but it's what I would do if an English person offered ME tea," I said.

Pouring the tea on the floor WOULD be like the Boston Tea Party. In case you haven't heard of it: In Boston, at the beginning of the Revolution, a crowd of grown-ups disguised as Indians sneaked onto English ships and dumped all the tea into the harbor. I think it's neat that our country had such a fun start — grown-ups dressing up like Indians and throwing things overboard! And I like the name Boston Tea Party, too. I didn't say any of that to Neil, though.

We brought him into our room and he stood in the middle of it, with his back very straight, turning his chin around and looking at everything quite coolly.

I was looking out the window at the rain when the front doorbell rang. I ran down, and it was Henry!

"My mother said I could only come in if your mother said it was okay with her," he said. "And she said to give your mother this note when you asked."

"Okay," I said.

I ran in. The two mothers were still just sitting there, talking — that's all my mother ever does when her friends come over: talk.

"It's Henry. Can he come in?"

I gave her the note.

"Excuse me," she said to Mrs. Grant.

She read it quickly, and then the two mothers looked at each other — I don't know if they used the secret code or whatever it is ladies use to tell each other things privately. I know they have one. (Once I called my mother and asked her to come get me at a friend's house. I told her NOT to tell them why. When she came, I listened to every word my mother said, and she didn't say anything about the reason; but at the end, the other mother said, looking relieved, "So THAT's what it was!" So I knew my mother told her, but I'd heard every word she said and I don't know *how* she told her.)

My mother said Henry was "a nice boy" and Mrs. Grant said Neil wasn't shy and then she laughed and said something I didn't quite understand.

"All right," my mother said (to me). "As long as all four of you play together, and ask before you go outside."

I ran back.

"She said yes!"

We ran upstairs. Neil was talking to Emmy, looking a little nicer than he had before. And when Henry and I were listing things we could do and trying to choose, he looked really interested, and after a while he said, "In England on rainy days people go down the stairs on trays. It's called indoor tobogganing."

That sounded fun to me.

"Let's try it!" I said. "We don't have any big trays — except the one my mother is using — but what about a box? There are plenty of those lying around!"

"A box going down stairs with people in it would be hard to control," Henry said. "And dangerous, too."

He looked at Neil kind of disapprovingly.

"I haven't actually done it," Neil said.

I still wanted to try it, but no one else did, and Henry kept saying more and more reasons against it. Finally I said, "Oh, all right! What about Sardines?"

"What's that?" Neil said eagerly, as though he thought it was going to be something exciting.

"Someone hides . . . when you find him, you get into the hiding place, too — IF you can do it without anyone else seeing you," I said, looking at Emmy. Once, when Peg was It, Emmy held out her arms and shouted "Peggy!" as soon as she saw her — right in front of all of us, even though no one else had seen Peggy! It was kind of funny, but still.

"That was when I was only five," Emmy said.

When it was my turn to hide, I ran, quietly, to the big barrel filled with crumpled-up paper I'd seen in the dining room. I boosted myself up with my arms (the way I do when I jump onto the kitchen counter), and then it was easy to lower my legs in quietly, so the paper wouldn't rustle.

I curled up like a cat; all I could see was the ceiling and the sides of the barrel. I could hear the others tramping around, and laughing and yelling. Something fell over with a loud crash.

Then I heard quick footsteps in the dining room. I looked up — and saw my mother staring down at me.

"Honestly, Libby!" she said. "No! No! Don't move!"

She grabbed me by one shoulder and one knee so hard that it hurt, and swung me out of the barrel and up into the air. Then she let go of me, fast — my feet banged the floor.

"You are the limit," she said. "Can't you ever be careful of anything?"

"But — what did I do?"

She just looked at me.

"Was there something in the barrel besides paper?" I said.

"The wildflower breakfast set."

I knew the one she meant. She put her hand in the barrel and took out a big ball of paper and held it in both hands. Without looking at me, she

From the wildflower breakfast set.

said, "This china was my grandmother's. I've never broken even one teacup handle."

Henry, Neil, and Emmy ran in. They stopped when they saw our mother and stood in the doorway staring at her with their mouths hanging open. Henry and Emmy know that our mother doesn't yell and doesn't hit and doesn't get mad. She wasn't yelling but she really was mad, everyone could see that.

"If ONE THING in that china barrel is broken —" She stopped; I waited, but she didn't say anything else.

"What?" I said. "What will happen?"

She didn't say anything.

"IS anything broken?" I said.

"I don't know."

"Well can't you look?" I said — I hate waiting for punishments, I'd rather just get it over with.

She didn't answer me; she just looked at the ball of paper in her hands — it was probably one of the china pieces.

"If anything is broken there's nothing I can do about it now," she said finally. She put the china piece (whatever it was) back in the barrel, very gently, without looking at me at all.

"But then when will I find out what my punishment is going to be?"

"You'll just have to wait until we come back from England and I unpack this barrel," she said, and went back to the living room.

Her grandmother gave her the breakfast set because she liked it so much, and she always washes it by hand, not in the dishwasher. Each piece has flowers painted on it, and she says they're realistic — that's one reason she liked them so much when she was a child. She liked flowers and china and dolls and things like that when she was a little girl. She wasn't a tomboy like me.

Slowly, I walked to the living room door to tell my mother I was sorry — she had looked so sad, and it *was* a pretty stupid thing to have done. But my mother's back was to the door, and when Mrs. Grant saw me, she looked almost as if she was scared. I didn't want to apologize in front of *her*.

So I went back to the dining room. Neil and Emmy were talking — he seemed shocked and she looked worried. Henry was peering curiously into the china barrel.

I looked into it, too.

"Maybe nothing's broken," Henry said. "It looks like there's a lot of padding in there, and you're pretty light."

That was nice of him; but I wondered what my father would do. My mother hardly ever punishes us. (Henry always says he wishes she could be our teacher, "because she'd always be saying 'I'll give you one more chance.'") My father does.

Chapter Four: "Bon Voyage!"

The first thing my father asked my mother about at dinner (we were having a family "Bon Voyage!" party for my father, with poppers from Chinatown as party favors) was the tea party, and she said, "I think it was interesting for everyone."

If that was some kind of code, my father didn't get it. No one said anything else about the tea party or the china barrel.

When we came downstairs the next morning, our parents were both up and dressed! (Usually on weekend mornings we get up way before they do.) My father was in his work clothes, and a suitcase was standing next to his brief-case. He looked really excited — he was leaping around my mother, laughing and trying to pick her up. She was shaking her head and kind of pushing him away but kind of not.

Party favors from Chinatown: When you pull the string, they explode with a loud noise and smell of gunpowder.

"Come and give me a kiss, kids," he said. "The next time you see me will be in England!"

"In London?" I said — I was excited, too, about going on the boat and everything.

"No, I'll meet you where the boat docks and we'll all take a train together to London."

That sounded fun, too — I was about to ask if we would walk down a gangplank and he would be standing at the bottom of it, waving to us — when Emmy started to cry. My father stood still and looked sad for a second.

"Aw, Em, don't cry," he said, picking her up. "It's not very long until November tenth."

"I bet that's the day the boat — the *Liberty*! — docks!" I said.

"Why can't we all go together?" Emmy said.

"I have to find a place for us to live, and a school for you and Libby, and your mother has to pack and get your passports and rent the house," he said, and looked at my mother eagerly. "Right, Sall?"

My mother nodded; she didn't look excited at all.

"Don't worry, you'll get it done, there's time," he said, putting Emmy down. Then he gave her a big hug and said it was time to leave. "So long, shorty! Be good!" he said to me, and he bent down for us all to kiss him.

After my father left, we didn't have dining room dinners anymore — we ate in the kitchen and our mother let us talk as much as we wanted. We got to miss school for our passport picture. People came to look at the house, and my mother's friends came over a lot to help — they brought their children, and we played with them, and she let The Gang play inside, too.

But one day, she said NO ONE ELSE COULD COME OVER UNTIL WE WERE DONE PACKING. We couldn't even go outside and play! She said, "Have you decided yet which three books or toys you're going to take?"

"Not quite," I said. I HAD been thinking about it, though. "*Peter Pan* (because it was my first favorite book) and *Little Women* (because it's my favorite book now), but I'm not sure about the third thing."

I was hesitating between my six-shooter and its holster (which I hoped would count as one thing) or a perfume bottle my grandmother had given me that had once belonged to a real princess. I

liked it because of that, and because of its color (dark green glass with a few tiny white leaves and real gold top) and shape. I was also thinking of *Grimm's Fairy Tales*, because it was the longest, thickest book I had, and I like fairy tales — especially "Rumpelstiltskin" and "One Eye, Two Eyes, and Three Eyes" (that little table that spreads itself with a white cloth and food!). It was a hard choice.

A picture from the fairy tale "East of the Sun and West of the Moon."

"I've ALMOST decided on *Grimm's Fairy Tales*," I said. Privately, I was also planning to bring my little metal horse: It was so small that I could put it in a pocket, or around my wrist with its chain bridle.

"Well, you can be thinking about it while you sort and pack your papers," my mother said, opening the big drawer where we keep our old drawings and stories.

"You need to throw out —," she hesitated, then took out two big piles, "about that many papers each."

She gave one pile to Emmy and one to me.

"I'll come back to check on you in fifteen minutes."

We sat down with our piles: When I found something of Emmy's, I handed it to her; when she found something of mine, she handed it to me, as usual. But usually our mother looks at the things with us. We all — including our mother — talk about what we find and other things, too; it's fun. But that day, she didn't look at anything, even after she said she would "supervise" (usually, that means she does most of whatever it is, but when we sort, she just watches).

She did sit down on the bed. But she kept jumping up to go pack things, and then running back in to hurry us along, instead of admiring our drawings and stories with us as usual.

She did look at one of Emmy's old drawings and listen to me read one of my silly witch stories out loud, though. Then I found an old paper-doll book.

PART OF THE SILLY WITCH
STORY I READ:

One day the Witch said, "I will fool those little kids. I'm hurrying."

And then she hurried down to the store. "Um," she said.

"What do you want?" said the ghost, for it was the ghost store.

"I want to buy some apples."

"Do you have to?"

"Yes I need them!" she shouted.

So he gave her a bag of rotten apples.

"For Pete's sake!" said the Witch. "Of all the crazy things . . ."

"Annie Oakley! I've been wondering where this was!" I said. "Remember, I got it for my birthday and I never cut out ONE outfit: look, they're all still in here. Even Annie Oakley is still here — where are the scissors?"

"I thought you didn't like paper dolls," our mother said. She does; sometimes she cuts them out with us. It's true that usually I don't: If you make a mistake cutting out their faces, they look funny; and the little tabs that hold on the clothes (and the clothes themselves) rip and fall off so easily.

"I like Annie Oakley," I said. The cover showed Annie riding a galloping horse with her elbows sticking out. Inside were cowboy boots and buckskin jackets and cowgirl skirts and gun holsters, not the usual paper-doll things. "Where are the scissors?"

"No!" our mother said. She hardly ever says no like that. "Tomorrow the movers are coming while you're in school and the next day we're leaving. *You need to do this now.*"

"Is tomorrow our last day of school?" I said, and she said it was.

The real Annie Oakley, who was the best shot in the West. She met her husband when she beat him in a shooting contest.

Chapter Five:
"Will You Miss Me?"

It was our last whole day and the very last day of school, Miss Jessup said anyone who wanted to could make a card for me. While she was passing out the paper, Henry said, "What will Libby do?"

"She can draw or write whatever she wants."

I decided to make a good-bye card for the class. I wondered how many people would make cards for me.

An ocean liner a boy drew.

I could tell that they were all coloring by the way their arms were moving. But even though I could see some of the drawings, I didn't know if they were cards for me. Even when they were done, I didn't know, because Miss Jessup collected them all.

"I'll give them to you at the end of the day, Libby," she said.

So I had to wait until we had put our chairs up and were standing on line, waiting for the bell. And then, finally, when we were walking out, she gave me a stack of cards — a thick stack.

It felt like most people had made me one! I flipped through them: I could tell right away that lots of the girls had. There were little pictures, all colored in. They had put their addresses on the back (Miss Jessup told them to do that) and "Love," after the messages and before their names. I was surprised that the girls liked me so much! Or maybe that's just how girls write?

I counted the cards: twenty. But there were twenty kids in the class. Could she have put my card in the pile by mistake? Or had I made a mistake counting?

I looked through more carefully and saw that even Miss Jessup had made a card! Hers didn't have a picture, just the school's address in small, neat handwriting. Inside, she had written:

Dear Libby,

Your English school will be different, and perhaps difficult. You have a good mind and many abilities: use them. Try your best, even in those subjects that do not appeal to you. And remember that while you are in a foreign land, you are a representative of America. You may, perhaps, be the only American your teachers and schoolmates will ever meet. Make your behavior embody the ideals that have made Americans throughout history proud of themselves and of our country.

With best wishes,
Minerva Jessup

That was nice of her!

Henry had drawn a picture of a boat with LIBERTY in big letters on the side. Inside, he'd written:

Libby

I will see you in six months. Write to me as soon as you get there and I will write back.

Your friend,
Henry Hart

Well, no BOY would sign a card "Love." I wouldn't either!

I counted the cards again. This time, too, it came out to twenty — so everyone had made one. I was reading them all in order when Henry came running up.

"Look."

He held out a fortune-catcher — but I couldn't choose anything, because the four squares at the top were blank. Then he opened it and inside I read:

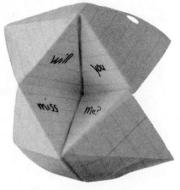

He closed it (fortune-catchers always look like little mouths closing and opening to me), and when he opened it the other way it said:

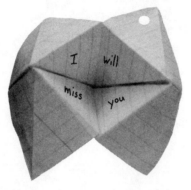

"Yes," I said out loud. "I'll miss you a lot."

We just looked at each other without saying anything, and then he ran across the street. After he crossed he turned around and waved and I waved back as hard as I could. I really, really like Henry. I *would* miss him — but it was good that he would miss me, too.

I looked at his card again, and decided to put it, and the fortune-catcher, inside *Grimm's Fairy Tales*, so they wouldn't get ripped on the voyage.

Chapter Six:
The Liberté

We were on our way: Everything was packed, our house was clean and locked, and the *Liberté* was moving slowly out of New York Harbor with us on the deck. My mother took Emmy's hand and told me to hold Willy's. She was already carrying Bubby.

"Really, Libby," she said, in a serious voice. "I don't want any of you out of my sight."

So we stood right next to her. We watched New York (all the skyscrapers) spread out in a line and little baby waves moving and sparkling below us.

And then above us — high above us — I saw the Statue of Liberty. I'd never realized before how HUGE it is. One arm was bigger than a tall building.

"Look, Willy, look!" I said. "The Statue of Liberty!"

Liberty! I raised my free arm up to the sky, the way she was holding hers, and held it there.

The Liberté *sailing out of New York Harbor. The big shape between the ship and the shore is the Statue of Liberty.*

"She was put there to welcome all the people from other lands who came to America," I said.

I thought of my grandparents coming from Finland, and my great-great somethings coming from England and Scotland and Norway, and of all the other people who came to America: thousands and thousands of them, all brave and adventurous and full of hope. And they were all welcomed. I felt very proud of them and of our country, proud to be an American.

Willy tugged at my hand and I looked down: He was saluting, too, with his free hand. He smiled proudly at me and I squeezed his hand and smiled back. Liberty!

By dinner, we were, I thought, out of America, and on the Atlantic Ocean — and even if where we were didn't count as a new country (my mother said we were "in international waters"), it felt like we were in one.

The Dining Salon was very fancy. Everyone had assigned tables, and a huge man — taller and bigger than my father and a little bit fat (but on him it didn't look bad to be fat because he was so big) — sat with us at ours.

He had a dark, proud, serious face. He sat very straight and square, like a king with his arms on his throne. But what was really fascinating was that he wore a huge feathered headdress — not like an Indian's: his was a kind of turban with big feathers of all different colors around it. He wore wonderful pale green robes that went down to the ground (I bent down under the tablecloth and looked).

I was wondering if he was a king, or at least a prince or chieftain, when my mother shook her head at me, just a little bit, but I knew that she meant, "It's rude to stare."

She had given us a little talk about manners before we left our cabin for the Dining Salon, and I knew that she really wanted us to be polite. It was hard, but I looked around the room and tried not to look back at him too often.

All the tables were round and covered with long, white table-cloths that seemed very thick. I asked the waiter questions whenever I could; the most interesting answer was: "When it gets rough, we pour water on the tablecloths to keep the dishes from sliding off the tables."

"When will that happen?" I said. He said it probably wouldn't; most crossings were calm. Still, I thought, it *might* happen on ours. I hoped it would.

After dinner, we went to our cabins. Emmy and I had a cabin to ourselves, which was very exciting.

"Be sure to keep the door locked," my mother said again when she kissed us good-night, "and don't unlock it for anyone but me." Her cabin — which Willy and Bubby were in, too — was right next door to ours. Still, it was pretty cool to have our own.

It was cozy, with just room for a little table and chair and a mirror (all screwed in), and another chair in a tiny alcove under the porthole. You could stand on the chair to look out the porthole — only it was shut with a round metal shutter, painted the same creamy white as the walls, and locked.

"Let's get in bed," I said. We had already decided to take turns sleeping in the top bunk, and the first night, it was mine. I climbed up into it: It had a lamp above the pillow so you could read in bed. I hung my little metal horse on the lamp by its bridle.

The sheets were thick and kind of scratchy: They didn't feel like our sheets at home at all. They were tucked in VERY tightly and I had to wriggle around for a long time before I felt comfortable.

"What are you doing?" Emmy said from the bottom bunk.

I hung my head over the side of the top bunk and looked down at her with my head upside down.

"Getting settled in."

I made a face and she made one back.

"What will we do tomorrow?" she said.

"Explore the ship."

"Don't you want to go in the playroom?"

The playroom had a baby-sitter in a white uniform and the kinds of toys that girlie-girls and very little children like. It was perfect for Willy: lots of blocks.

"You can — I'd rather explore."

As soon as breakfast was over, we did.

First, we ran up to the deck (our cabin and the Dining Salon were below the deck). It was narrow and crowded with grown-ups lying in deck chairs, or walking slowly, or playing a really boring game kind of like hopscotch, or just standing around, leaning their elbows on the wall that circled the deck — this was painted a creamy white, like everything else on the ship. They were looking out — at what? What could they see? All I could see was sky and water. I jumped up, to see more, but there was nothing out there but sky and water.

Stewards bustled around, bringing blankets and snacks to the grown-ups and watching us suspiciously. Once, in a place where there was a little space, I skipped a few skips, and one shouted at me.

So, the deck was pretty boring. We decided to explore the rest of the ship. I ran down the first empty staircase we came to. No one stopped me. I ran back up, then ran down my favorite way. I grabbed the banister three steps below me tightly with one hand, then jumped SIX steps at once. I sort of run and jump and leap all at the same time — it's almost like flying, with a short pause in between jumps to grab the banister again. Before the very bottom, you let go and bend your knees to land on the ground with a huge thud.

I ran back to the top and did it again: "Emmy, try running and jumping down more than one step at a time! Just grab the banister tightly and jump!" I said. "It's really fun — like this, watch!"

She did; it WAS really fun and we both laughed a lot.

When we got sick of that, we explored. The ship was so big that there were lots of empty places — there just weren't any on the deck itself. But BELOW the deck, there were stairs and ladders to climb up and down, and lots and lots of halls: wide ones (main halls) and narrower ones (side halls) and all of them had shiny, slippery floors, perfect for running and sliding and chasing each other. Here is a letter about it that I wrote to my class but never mailed:

Wed. Nov. 26, 1958

French Line
· LIBERTÉ ·

To The class

I'm having a pretty good time on the ship. Exscept there are a few troubles. One is that if you go to a pupet show it's in french. Another is that if you take a Bath. Wicth you would rather not because you are left all alone with the thougth that someone may come right in. But then there are fun things one is that you can go to the movie's and every other day the movie is in English. And some times this is fun and Some times it isn't. All most all the stureds and bell boy's speack French. Now I want to tell you something funny that happened. well my sister was chasing me down one of the main hall's and I was stupid a nuff to run down a side hall.

But I did. Then when we got
to the end she gave me a litte
push and we fell right into a man's
room, you see his door was unlooked.
Then we all started laghing even
the man. Then when I got my breth
I said oh I'm every sory. But he just
smiled and said thats all right. I'm
glad he was a citasin of the U.SA.
Becays then he wouldn't think every
body in our contrey was awful. And
this is true.

Your, Freind

Libby Koponen

I never found out where the man at our dining table was from, or whether he was a king or what. My mother said that it wouldn't be polite to bring a map into the dining room so he could point to his country, and that it would be *very* rude to try to talk to him with sign language. But I DID learn why iron ships don't sink — one of the bellboys told me. They're not solid metal: they have huge spaces filled with air built into them — so much air that the ship becomes light enough to float on water, just as a big balloon attached to a basket full of people is light enough to float in the air. And even though I never found out anything about the king (or chieftain or prince), it was neat that people like that lived in the world and I had met one.

Chapter Seven:
In London

When I woke up I didn't know where I was at first. Then, I remembered: I was in London.

I looked around. My bed was in the corner, under the window. Emmy's, Bubby's, and Willy's beds were in a row on the opposite wall.

The window was high on the wall, with black iron bars on it, and behind the bars a black iron fence with spaces between each pointed rod. There were no splotches of sun on the wall or the floor, just steady gray light and what little I could see of the sky (the room was in a basement) was gray, too.

"Emmy? Willy? Bubby?" I whispered.

They didn't answer: still asleep, probably. They had all

The window and its view, as they looked from my bed.

been asleep when we'd arrived, too: a grown-up named Jill who was going to be living with us had opened the door and helped carry them and our suitcases down to this room.

The suitcases were still on the floor, with their baggage tags on.

We'd carried them down the gangplank — even Willy carried one in the hand that wasn't holding mine. The gangplank was exactly the same as the New York gangplank: just a short metal bridge with solid metal walls, painted the same creamy color as the deck walls.

But I could see right away that we were in a foreign country. The light was different — darker. It wasn't just that it was a cloudy afternoon: The sky seemed heavier and closer to the ground than it did in America. I wasn't sure I liked it. It *was* exciting, though, and it made me curious. As I said, "If even the SKY is different, just think what London will be like!"

I looked up again at the window in our bedroom: Outside, it looked like the day hadn't even really started yet, it was so dark. The air felt damp, too, the way it does very early in the morning, before the sun comes up.

I got up and opened my suitcase, and then I decided to wake Emmy up. After all, it was our first day! She'd want to get ready for school early, too.

Chapter Eight:
St. Vincent's School

Jill, not my mother, took Emmy and Willy and me to school; Bubby stayed at home with my mother. (My mother had said we could stay home, too, but my father laughed and said there was no jet lag when you went on an ocean liner, and that he'd told the school we'd be there that morning.)

We didn't walk: we went in a taxi — it was black, and square, and very old-fashioned.

I pressed my face to the window. London seemed old-fashioned, too. The sky was still dark gray, and most of the buildings, even the stores, looked like houses, not skyscrapers. Most were dirty-white — sometimes so dirty they were almost black — stone. There were lots of little parks; they looked wet and dark, too — dark green grass, bare dark trees.

The only colors were on the advertisements and buses. The buses were a bright, cheerful red, twice as tall as American buses. We'd seen them the night before, too (with both rows of windows glowing yellow), and my father said they were called "double-deckers." I looked eagerly for more: I liked their color (bright red) and their shape, too. They were VERY cheerful.

The school looked just like the narrow, dirty-white houses on either side of it, except for a small metal sign that said: ST. VINCENT'S SCHOOL.

We went into a little hallway; two women were already standing there, smiling at us.

"I'm Mrs. Reed, the headmistress," the older one said, still smiling. "And you're the three little Americans. Who's the eldest?"

I didn't like her smile (too many teeth) or the way she talked ("*little* Americans"), but I answered.

"I am."

"Come with me, dearie," she said. "Miss Reed will sort out the others."

None of us said a word. Emmy and I made a quick face at each other (she didn't like the Reeds, either, I could tell). Willy stared after me with wide-open eyes: he looked horrified. I ran back and gave him a quick hug, and then I followed Mrs. Reed upstairs.

She opened a door and said to a roomful of children, "She's new — from America."

She left, and the children and I looked at each other.

They all wore white shirts and gray sweaters and navy-blue ties — even the girls had ties — and over the sweaters they had navy-blue jackets. The boys wore gray wool shorts and the girls wore skirts, and they all wore knee socks. The sweaters and skirts and shorts weren't exactly the same, just the same colors; but all the jackets were exactly alike.

I was wearing a green plaid jumper.

"Do you live on a huge ranch?" a girl said eagerly.

"No."

"Do you have your own gun?" a boy said. I could tell that he meant a real gun, not a toy. My six-shooter was in America, anyway, packed up in some box, because I'd brought *Grimm's Fairy Tales*.

"No," I said.

"Your own horse?"

"No."

"Rum!" someone said.

I guessed that meant "weird" and I was right — I asked Jill about it later. *I* thought it was weird that they all acted as though America was like the Wild West on TV. Then an older boy with a thin face and blue-silver eyes (I guess they were mainly pale blue, with glints of silver) said, "What's your name?"

"Libby. What's yours?"

He didn't answer. Instead, he laughed. One of the girls said Libby was "an odd sort of name."

"Libby drink Libby's!" the boy with the glinting eyes said, and laughed again.

The kids all started playing again and then an even older boy who was holding a little book said, "Can you spell?"

"Yes," I said.

"Women," he said.

"W-o-m-i-n," I said.

"*E*-n," he said, and everyone laughed. I realized that he had meant *Are you a GOOD speller?* I am a very bad speller, but you probably already know that from the letter I wrote on the *Liberté*.

No one else said anything to me, so I sat down and watched the kids running around until the teacher came in and the older boys went out and the other kids ran to their seats. They didn't sit down: They stood straight behind them, as though they were in the army standing at attention.

So I stood at attention, too. The teacher raised her hand and they sang a song that had the same tune as "My Country 'Tis of Thee." It went:

> *God save our gracious Queen,*
> *Long live our noble Queen,*
> *God save the Queen.*
> *Send her victorious,*
> *Happy and glorious,*
> *Long to reign over us,*
> *God save the Queen!*

Then they sat down. They folded their hands, bent their necks, closed their eyes, and said, all together:

> *I am the child of God,*
> *I ought to do his will,*
> *I can do what he tells me to*
> *And with his help I will.*

Then they sat up and the teacher looked at me.

"You must be the American," she said. "Come here, Elizabeth." She gave me three little books — all very thin — an old-fashioned pen, and a bottle of ink. I was looking at the pen when she said it was time for spelling.

"Curious," she said, and the girl next to me wrote in her little book. But when I tried to write in mine, my pen just made scratches on the paper.

"You must fill it UP!" the teacher said, and everyone laughed.

They were all looking at me, waiting.

I opened the pen: The bottom unscrewed, too, and inside it, attached to the point, was a little rubber tube. I dipped the point into the ink, then squeezed the tube gently — ink went in, you could see it and feel it filling the tube. When the tube was hard and full, I squished it — ink squirted out.

"Honestly, Elizabeth!" It was the teacher. She sounded annoyed. "Haven't you ever seen a pen before?"

She was just being sarcastic, I think. Anyway I didn't want to tell her that I really hadn't. I just filled the pen up again as quickly as I could. A few people

Instead of having a smooth, straight point like a pencil, their pens had a big metal thing that ended in a point. The pointed metal thing, I found out later, is called a nib.

snickered; the teacher gave me a dirty look and then said, still in a sarcastic voice, "If you're quite finished, Elizabeth?"

Then she said the next word.

When we were done, she collected the books and corrected them — I, she said, had gotten almost everything wrong. It's true that I'm a terrible speller.

The metal desk was cold on my arms, and soon I felt cold all over, especially my hands and feet. I looked at the desk — it was very pale green, splotched with black. I didn't like either color.

In the middle of the morning we went downstairs to another classroom; it was full of little children. Emmy ran next to me, and Miss Reed had Willy (who seemed to be the youngest of all) on her lap. He was smiling a little uncertainly.

I waved to him and then stood close to Emmy while Mrs. Reed passed out small glass bottles of milk with silver paper tops. At the top, the milk was all yellow (cream) — the kids shook the bottles before they drank the milk.

"Here's your nice milk, dearie," Mrs. Reed said to me. "Mind you don't spill it."

Emmy told me that this was their classroom, and that they did their lessons out loud, sort of singing. She said Miss Reed sat in the front of the room holding a big ruler like a baton and singing (and all the kids sang along): "One and one are TWO, Two and two are FOUR, . . ." Emmy thought this was very funny: As she told me about it, she kept stopping to laugh. I wasn't sure what I thought, but it didn't seem funny to me.

After "elevenses" (that's what the snack was called), we had more lessons; they were more interesting than what we did in school in America. We read a real book, *The Borrowers,* and wrote a composition about it in the thin little books (these were called exercise books) in ink. I liked writing with an old-fashioned pen and ink: Everything came out so thick and black.

Then we had English history. I looked all through the history book, but I couldn't find anything at all about the Revolution.

I decided not to ask about it. Everyone, even the teacher, laughed when I talked — not in a nice way, as though they thought it was funny, but in a mean way. They laughed as though there was something wrong with me, or the way I talked.

But what? What was wrong with the way I talked?

Nothing, I thought. I just sounded different because I had an American accent and they had English ones. Probably they would stop doing it when they got used to me. After all, I thought, it was only the middle of the afternoon on the first day. School would get better; they would get used to me and start liking me soon.

Chapter Nine:
One Good Thing

They didn't. After a few days, the only person who talked to me at all was Norman Capp, the boy who'd asked my name the first day. And I wished he wouldn't.

Whenever I tried to start a conversation with the others — in the classroom in the morning, at the milk break, or at lunch — they made fun of my accent. If I tried to play in a game, they said I couldn't. So at the milk break and lunch I talked only to Emmy, and in the classroom, I sat at my desk and (if I had a book) read.

I often thought of Pat's words: "Maybe they'll say 'Uh! American girls!'" — that was smart of Pat.

One morning I was sitting at my desk reading as usual; and as usual, everyone ignored me until Norman Capp came in. I hoped that he would leave me alone.

"Libby drink Libby's!" he said, and everyone laughed. "Libby's" is a kind of milk they have in England; there were advertisements all over London that said DRINK LIBBY'S.

Then he jumped up on top of my desk and sang, as he did every morning. When he danced, he jumped and hopped all over the desk with his toes turned out — he looked silly, but everyone laughed at *me.* This is what he sang: "Libby there is milk for you! Nice and fresh, creamy too."

He sang it over and over; the other kids laughed and laughed. I just sat there — what could I say? In America I never THOUGHT about what I was going to say, I just said it. When you think before-hand, it's hard to say anything. So I didn't.

"Look how narrow and slanted her eyes are," someone — a girl — said.

"Ridiculous — like a blue-eyed Chinese," said another girl.

I folded my arms across my chest and thought about Daniel Boone being tortured by Indians.

Do you know that story? It's true — it happened in pioneer times. After the Indians captured his two sons, Daniel Boone ran af-ter them — but by the time he caught up with them, the Indians had already killed the two boys. Then they tortured Daniel Boone, but no matter what they did to him, he didn't make one sound or move one muscle in his face. The Indians rewarded his courage by letting him live.

I admire Daniel Boone; I'm proud that I'm an American like him.

"Especially with that short straight hair and ugly fringe that goes straight across her forehead."

A "fringe" is what they call bangs. Mine are cut in a very straight line, and it's true that compared to the kids in the class — who all looked kind of alike, with round eyes — mine are kind of odd-looking — narrow and slanted. It's because my father's ancestors are all Finns; but in America no one minded. In America, practically everyone looks different from everyone else, and it's okay. That's one thing America is about and one reason we fought the Revolution.

Then someone said, "Miss Bromley!" (that was the teacher) and Norman Capp went out and we stood at attention as Miss Bromley came in.

Their money was very different from ours. It was divided up into pounds (twenty shillings), shillings (twelve pennies), and pence (pennies). There were more coins than in America: a half-crown (two shillings and sixpence), a florin (two shillings), a shilling (twelve pennies), a sixpence (six pennies), a threepenny bit (three pennies), a tuppence (two pennies), a penny, and a ha'penny (half penny). All the coins said, "God save the Queen" in Latin.

Then they all sang "God Save the Queen." After the song, while everyone was sitting down, Miss Bromley looked at me and said, "Elizabeth, you weren't singing. Don't you know the words to 'God Save the Queen' by now?"

Of course, I did. I said, "I don't sing it because I'm an American, and we don't believe in kings and queens. We believe in liberty and justice for all — that's what the Revolution and the Boston Tea Party were about. I'll stand up, but I won't sing."

And if you try and make me, I won't do it, I thought. She just stared at me and I stared right back, thinking, I won't sing that song even if you hit me with your ruler (they did that to kids there). *I won't do it and you can't make me.* But I didn't say anything; I just stared at her. After a while, she looked down at her desk and said, "Very well, then, stand but don't sing."

I hated school, I hated London, I hated living in England, but she couldn't make me sing a song to their queen. That was one good thing, at least.

Chapter Ten:
Writing to Henry

Another good thing was the ride home. I came home by myself (Emmy's and Willy's classes got out earlier than mine, and they went home with Jill). When I left school the day I said I wouldn't sing it was almost dark.

I walked to the Underground and waited for my train right next to the UNDERGROUND sign. I liked how cheerful the Underground signs were — huge squares of white, taking up almost the whole wall, with a big bright red circle, and in the middle of the circle a blue bar with the name of the stop in white letters.

I liked the names of the stops, too: Lancaster Gate and Queensway — being in a country where they had a real queen and real castles was like being in a nursery rhyme or fairy tale. And I liked the train — they called it the tube and it was shaped like a tube, with walls that curved out at the sides and then up into the low ceiling. People sat or stood very close together, but no one talked. Sometimes grown-ups smiled at me. The lights were a warm yellow color and the train was warm, too; I was never cold on the Underground. I watched the people reading, and read the advertisements, and each time we stopped, I looked out the window, carefully watching the signs so I wouldn't miss my stop: Queensway.

When I got off and walked up the stairs to the street, it was completely dark: The sky was black, the street lights were on. I liked walking along Bayswater Road, because I walked along the edge of Kensington Gardens. I looked through the fence at the formal paths and old trees, imagining Peter Pan playing there. (My parents had given me a book about that part of his life, *Peter Pan in Kensington Gardens*.)

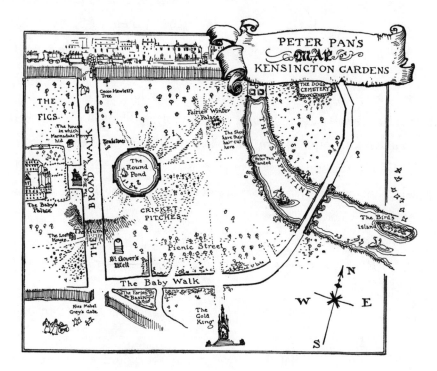

A map of Kensington Gardens from the book Peter Pan in Kensington Gardens.

When I turned onto our street, the lights were on in all the houses. I always like to see lighted windows when I'm outside in the dark: The rooms look so snug and safe.

At our house, Emmy's face was against the window by the front door: She was always there waiting for me, and I liked that, too. When she saw me, she waved, and when she disappeared, I knew she was unlocking the door.

We ran downstairs to our room, which Jill called "the nursery." Usually as soon as I got home we had a meal called tea: brown bread cut in quarters with chocolate spread, which is like chocolate syrup but thicker and not so sweet, and apples cut up into slices on plates. In England they don't bite into the whole apple.

But that day the table didn't have a tablecloth on it — Emmy had been drawing on it. Bubby was playing with her white china horses, and Willy was building a tower with books. Jill was knitting. She usually wore big, baggy, beige or pale green sweaters; she was knitting another one when I came in.

"Where's tea?" I said.

"Mommy and Daddy aren't going to the theater tonight," Emmy said.

"You're having dinner with Mummy and Daddy tonight," Jill said at the same time.

Then she said that since I was home, she would go upstairs and "make herself tidy" — she was going out that night, she said. She stood up and pulled her skirt down; her pale legs bulged out of it and out of her tan boots. Then she patted her tight black curly hair, told me to "mind the others," and left.

I got my pen and Quink (a kind of ink) and some paper and started to write.

"What are you writing?" Emmy said.

I didn't answer.

"A story?"

"No, a letter."

"To who?"

I didn't answer, and she leaned across the table.

"Dear Henry," she read out loud. "Why not TO Henry?"

I explained that you always started letters with "Dear." Then I said, "Now don't read any more — maybe I'll read it to you when I'm done, but I can't write with you reading every word as I go along."

I was still writing when our mother came in. She was wearing the new pink suit I'd helped her pick out, and she looked really pretty; I felt proud of how pretty she looked. She looked different than she looked in America: her hair was longer and softer — it curled around her shoulders instead of tightly all over her head. Also she smiles more. In America, she never seemed to have any fun. But in London she does: she and my father go to the theater a lot, and sometimes they go out to dinner, and sometimes they go dancing. Then she gets really dressed up, in a black skirt that swirls around, and she puts per-fume behind her ears (it's called Arpège and Daddy gave it to her. It has an expensive, very grown-up scent).

"You look really pretty, Mommy," I said.

She kind of shook her head, in an embarrassed way, and smiled. Her smile always was pretty.

"What are you writing?" she said.

"A letter to Henry."

She held out her hand and I gave it to her — she read it to herself and then she said, "There's an awful lot in here about not being able to wear your blue jeans, and missing your —," she kind of hesitated, "six-shooter. Don't you think that's kind of boring, honey?"

"But I *do* miss wearing blue jeans. I HATE having to wear skirts and dresses all the time."

"I know — you've said that — but imagine if someone you knew had moved to Japan, and you wanted to know what Japan was like, and the letter kept saying, 'And I can't wear my red sneakers.'"

Henry would understand how I felt — he always got it. And he never thought I was boring. At least — he never had before. But that didn't mean he never would. I'd never been unpopular before, either, and now I was. I read the letter to myself.

"I guess it is kind of boring," I said. "I'll write it over."

"But not now — it's time for dinner."

The dining room had one big window that looked out onto a small square of gray cement and dark walls. We had dinner at a long oval table that was really too big for our family. Our father sat at one end (it was so dark, and the table was so long, that it was hard to see him). Our mother sat at the other end, with me next to her, Emmy between me and my father, and Willy and Bubby across from us.

There was a chandelier that didn't give out much light over the table, and a tiny fireplace behind my father. During dinner, my parents talked to each other as usual. The only interesting part was when my father was telling her about "rhyming slang." He said that someone named Norman used it a lot and sometimes he, Daddy, didn't get it.

"Today he threw something on my desk and —" Daddy said the next part imitating the man's voice and accent and expression — Daddy's really good at imitating people, "— 'ere, 'av a butcher's at this.'"

"What did that mean?" I said.

"'Here, have a look at this.' 'Butcher's hook' means 'look.'"

"Is it code?" I said.

"Slang," Daddy said. "In rhyming slang, instead of saying a word, they say something that rhymes with it: 'wife' is 'trouble and strife.'" (He looked at my mother and laughed.) "But when they only say the part that doesn't rhyme, it can be hard to understand."

"What are some other ones?" I said.

My father made a face — he makes faces a lot when he talks — and said, "'Septic tank' is 'Yank' — short for Yankee, an American."

"And 'apples and pears' means stairs," my mother said.

"And 'Mable, Mable' could be table!" I said excitedly.

"Finish your dinner and don't talk so much," he said.

After a while I stopped listening. I thought about England, and how everything seemed to come out of a rhyme or a story — "Yank" was probably from the song "Yankee Doodle." (So they DID know about the Revolution! That proved it!)

At dessert, my father asked if any of us had learned anything interesting. I answered first.

"I learned that they used to make children pull carts in coal mines and clean the soot out of chimneys, because the tunnels and chimneys were too small for grown-ups to crawl into," I said. There was a picture of a chimney sweep in our history book — he looked about five! They're not very nice to children in this country, are they?"

The English made up the words to "Yankee Doodle" and sang it to insult the American soldiers in the Revolution: "doodle" meant "fool."

Yankee Doodle went to town, riding on a pony,
Stuck a feather in his hat and called it macaroni.
Yankee Doodle, keep it up! Yankee Doodle, dandy!
Mind the music and the step and with the girls be handy!

But the Americans sang their own words right back at the redcoats:

Yankee Doodle is the tune Americans delight in;
Twill do to whistle, sing, or play and just the thing for fightin'.
Yankee Doodle, keep it up! Yankee Doodle, dandy!
Mind the music and the step and with the girls be handy!

"They have laws against that sort of thing now," my mother said.

"But it would never have happened at all in America, because we had the Revolution."

My father laughed and asked how I knew that.

"Well, I don't KNOW—but I bet they thought it was better for chimneys to be dirty than for kids to be chimney sweeps. Or maybe they just had bigger chimneys! Our fireplace in America was big."

"Was that because of the Revolution, too?" he said in a teasing voice.

"It's not funny!" I said—saying anything else would just make him laugh more. He doesn't really understand about the Revolution.

Emmy said, "We learned this: 'Nouns are just the names of things, Like birds and beasts and cats and kings . . .'"

I forget the rest — she chanted it in the singsong way they did at school, imitating Mrs. Reed keeping time with her ruler, and Willy joined in. We all laughed, and then my mother started to clear the table, and we went to our room.

I read in bed until my mother came in to get the others ready for bed and read a story. While she was reading, I took Henry's last letter out of the white box and held it in my hand, and I thought about what I could say in my letter that wouldn't be boring. I decided to tell about the Underground, and the red buses, and the soldiers in their red uniforms (*real* redcoats!) guarding the palaces. Henry was interested in soldiers. I'd tell him how stalwart they looked, no matter what happened or what anyone said or did; I was interested in that, too.

The soldiers guarding Buckingham Palace always walked back and forth, back and forth, just outside the fence, and no matter what anyone watching them said or did, they never changed their expressions or said a word back. Except once, my mother told us (she read about it in the paper), an American tourist — a grown-up — walked next to one of these soldiers and shouted insults at him for over two hours, trying to make him talk or look at her. But he wouldn't — until finally, after more than two hours, he kicked her in the shin. After that the soldiers marched inside the palace fence.

Chapter Eleven: Another Good Thing

I wasn't very stalwart the next morning. The day started with one of those happy dreams I have *just* before it's time to get up, only this one was very real.

In the dream, it was a sunny fall afternoon in Pleasantville. Kenny and Peg and Pat and Emmy and I were in our front yard, hula-hooping under the trees. The air was thin and the light was pale. It was hot and I could feel the sun on my face and dead leaves scratching my socks; the leaves above me blazed yellow and orange and red; I could see bright blue sky and sunlight shining through them all, especially the yellow ones.

When I first woke up I thought I *was* at home in America, and I was happy — until I remembered.

I was in London.

I was in London, in the basement room with the black bars on the windows. In London, where when it wasn't raining it was gray — gray all day and dark by the time I got out of school. London. I felt heavy and gray, like the buildings and the sidewalks and the sky and the air.

I had the dream every morning. It was always exactly the same, and I always woke up happy from it, until I remembered where I really was.

I was in London. One morning I looked up at the heavy gray sky (what you could see of it through all the black bars) and almost started to cry. *I never cry.* I didn't even cry when I slit my knee open playing baseball and had to have thirteen stitches! I had to do something.

There was a high bookshelf in the hallway outside our room. I looked up at the books and then carried a chair in from the dining room and stood on it to choose. The paint was peeling, and the heat pipes near the ceiling were dusty and so were the books. There were books for children and grown-ups; I took down some of each and started reading.

The one I read first was about five sisters whose mother really wanted them to get married, and it was called *Pride and Prejudice*. One of the sisters (named Lizzy — her real name was Elizabeth, like mine) was lively and charming; she was her father's favorite. She had very arched eyebrows and the question marks in the book were arched, too, and the author said Lizzy talked

" She is . . . not handsome enough to tempt *me*."
[*see page 10*]

This is from the first book I read.

"archly" — it all fit together, and I liked that. The mother was very childish and silly (she was so ridiculous that she made me laugh, and I liked that, too) and the father made jokes about everything, and because Lizzy was smarter than all her sisters he thought she was great; all the men liked her.

This is what I always did on sight-seeing trips when we got to the sight my parents wanted to see.

I loved that book. I brought it everywhere with me. I brought it to school and read it there, and on the Underground, and at home I read without stopping from the time I got home from school until dinner, and then from dinner until I went to sleep.

If they made me get out of the car, this is what I did.

On weekends, when my parents took us on sight-seeing trips, I'd stay in the car, reading it. If my father made me get out of the car, I'd sit down next to it and go on reading.

As soon as I finished one book, I started another. After a while I read mostly books about girls going to boarding school: There were lots of those books in the apartment, and I loved them.

The girls in those books slept in a room with other girls their own age and ate together and had lessons together. Usually in them a new girl came, and the other girls made fun of her and teased her and didn't like her at first — and then she did something heroic and everyone liked her a lot.

Or sometimes the girls had adventures together: The adventure usually started at night with someone putting on her dressing gown and getting a torch (that's what they call a flashlight). I was surprised that they always had torches with batteries and bulbs that worked; each time they'd get the torch I'd wonder if this time the battery or bulb would be dead, but it never was.

And there was always a scene of a midnight feast: In the middle of the night, they would get up, put on their dressing gowns, light their torches, and spread food on a blanket.

So that was another good thing, reading. I read like that until one Saturday Jill took us to a toy store.

Chapter Twelve:
The Dolls

Two of the dolls, as they looked when they were in the store.

It was more like a room in an old-fashioned house than a toy store.

The best things were in a long wooden case with a glass top and glass front. Inside were dolls — not big dolls, but dollhouse dolls. I never liked dolls in America: Their faces didn't look real at all.

But these were not like any dolls I'd ever seen — their faces had real expressions. They were about as long as my fingers: the children as long as my little finger, the grown-ups the size of my middle finger. We looked through the case for a long time, until the man behind it asked, very politely, if we'd like him to take any of the dolls out for us so we could "see them properly." He talked to us just as though we were grown-up ladies and he was a grown-up gentleman — he almost bowed!

The doll Libby, when she was very old, almost falling apart — I took the picture while I was writing this book so you could see her.

We pointed to the ones we liked best, and he set them down on the counter and said we could hold them, and we thanked him and did hold them.

The legs AND arms bent and so did the bodies, so you could put them in any pose. Their feet were in metal shoes, so they didn't bend, and their heads didn't bend, but the necks did. They would even be able to RIDE. We looked and looked.

Finally, I picked out a boy with shorts and brown hair and kind of a sweet but mischievous expression. I decided to get him and a girl with a very short dress (yellow) and short curly brown hair. She had a sweet, wistful face. I got her and named her Emmy.

Emmy got a girl and a boy, too. The girl had kind of an angry expression, curly hair, and a white dress with red and blue lines that made squares. She was a little taller than my Emmy; Emmy named her girl Libby.

There was also a baby with long, curly blonde hair and a long pink nightgown — but we didn't have enough money to get her, or any grown-ups (the grown-ups cost more, and besides, we could wait to get them). And the things they had to go WITH the dolls! All kinds of furniture, with drawers that really opened; a pink telephone with a tiny dialer that really turned. . . . But we could get them later; the important thing was that we had the dolls. I could hardly wait to get home and play with them.

Once we had the dolls, every day was fun — at least after school.

The mothers were both very frivolous: They spent all their time going shopping and talking about clothes and going to the theater. The fathers were very quiet and spent most of their time reading (we made books by cutting out the pictures of books advertised in magazines and pasting them onto folded-up paper). None of the parents paid any attention to the adventurous children, so the kids could do whatever they wanted.

There was also a crotchety old grandfather, who had black-and-white-checked trousers and a black tailcoat, a white beard, curly white hair, and glasses. He was very excitable (sometimes he got drunk and waved the green wine bottle around). There was also a doll with gray hair and a gray nurse's uniform

THE BEST THINGS WERE:

- a wooden case about half the length of my little finger. The outside was polished, shining wood; inside, it was lined with green baize (that's like velvet, only rougher) and divided into three tiny compartments holding tiny silver knives, spoons, and forks.

- a dark green wine bottle with a cork and a label you could really read. It came with a set of matching real glass wine glasses.

- a silver tray (real silver) with two real glasses.

- a silver-colored toaster with two pieces of toast: you could take the toast in and out, and there was a black rubber knob on the side that you pulled up and down to make the toast go in and pop out.

- a china tea set with tiny dark pink flowers on everything: a round tray, teapot, creamer, sugar bowl, and two cups and saucers. The flowers have faded away, so now it's plain white.

and a crabby face and wire glasses; she looked after the children when their parents were out, which was most of the time.

The parents and nurse all spoke in English accents (though since the fathers hardly ever talked, they didn't really count). The grandfather's accent was sort of English and sort of Scottish; the children all had American accents.

The dolls wrote letters to each other on tiny pieces of paper with tiny printing — we made envelopes by folding paper and then gluing the flaps. Usually the mothers wrote the letters.

A letter from one of the mother dolls to the other mother doll:

> Darling: SUCH a bother! We're going to a ball and I don't have a THING to wear — I must go to London and get some new gowns. Would you like to come? Nursey can look after the children, of course. Ring me as soon as you get this: I hope the Post Office delivers it promptly. They're getting so slow and lazy, like servants!
>
> Your friend,
> Sally Koponen.

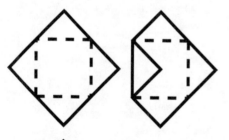

To make a doll envelope, cut a small square of paper, then fold in three of the corners and tape it, like this.

I read their letters to each other out loud in the proper accent for the person. Then, after I'd read the letter out loud, the dolls would do something.

Our favorite was to have the two mothers go shopping

or to the theater in London. Then the children could go into the forest, where they would always end up at the witch's house. It was sort of like "Hansel and Gretel" (only the dolls were never tricked by the witch!). We knew that we were copying the story, but we still liked to do it. And we didn't JUST copy, we made it funny. I think in the real story

"Hansel and Gretel," from an old book.

it's funny when Hansel and Gretel eat the gingerbread house — that their first reaction when they see a house is to start eating it, especially when the bird has just told them not to! Our children did even funnier things.

Emmy was fun to play dolls with — we hardly ever played alone with each other in America, but she was different in London. She acted different — she never talked in baby talk or fake-cried, and she did funny things when we were working the dolls. ("Working" is what we called moving them and making them talk; of course, she worked her dolls and I worked mine.)

We wished and wished that the dolls were alive, and sometimes we pretended that they *were* alive and that they just ACTED like dolls. One day when I came home from school Emmy told me that she had sneaked back into our room very quietly and . . .

"I saw all the dolls running back to their places," she said.

I wanted to believe her, and I almost did. I could picture Libby and Emmy running really fast and then lying down exactly where we had left them — but I knew it couldn't be true. I wondered a lot if Emmy really thought it was, but I couldn't ASK. It would be like asking someone if they still believed in Santa Claus. What if they did? So I didn't say anything. And when, sometimes, she said, "That wasn't where we left her!" I didn't argue, either.

Anyway, everything was better after we got the dolls, even school; until the six months were almost up — and we found out we were staying in England for another year.

Chapter Thirteen:
Something Big

When Daddy told us, Emmy and I could hardly believe it. We just looked at him, and then he said, "Aw, Em, don't cry. It's only a year."

ONLY a year! ONLY! It was easy for *him* to say that! He loved London. But we hated it. Only a year! — as if he was asking us to wait fifteen minutes (though even that's a long time when you want to go NOW). "Only a year." What a stupid thing to say!

I ran to my room and slammed the door. ONLY a year!

Then, when I was sure no one could hear me, I did something I hardly ever do (and didn't want to do then), because I was so disappointed and angry, too. ONLY a year! More than twice as long as we'd been here already before we could go home!

I was still crying when my mother came in to put the others to bed.

After she'd turned out the light, she came over to my bed. I could feel her sitting down on the edge of it before she gave my back a little pat.

"Do you hate it here that much?" she said in her gentlest voice. I didn't answer; I can't cry and talk at the same time. But I did make myself stop crying.

"Daddy and I thought you weren't very happy in London. We've been thinking about that, and talking to our friends here, and we thought you might be happier in the country. How would you like to go to a boarding school in the country?"

I thought of all the books about girls going to boarding school. It DID sound fun — and exciting, too.

I sat up.

"Could Emmy come too?"

"Well — six is a little young for boarding school," my mother said.

"She's almost seven. And in *The Girls of Rose Dormitory* the heroine's little sister was only five and she was at the school. So were other kids her age." (Though they were called "the babies.")

But when I asked Emmy, she didn't want to go, even when I told her that some schools in the stories had their own horses and the girls could ride them.

"That's in a book, not real life," she said.

"Things that happen in books happen in real life, too!" I said. "I bet that IS true!"

"Well even if it is I think we should all stay together."

But the more I thought about it, the better I liked the idea of going. Boarding school DID sound fun in the stories, and almost anything would be better than London. And if I found a really good school, one with horses, Emmy might change her mind. As my mother said, "Maybe when she's a little older."

My mother and I had lots of time to talk because it was vacation (they called it the Easter holidays even though it wasn't Easter yet), and we went to look at boarding schools almost every day.

They were empty, because it was the holidays, so of course that made them different from the books. But they didn't LOOK like the schools in the books, either, or at least not at all the way I had imagined those schools.

In real life, the rooms were little, and dark; and the people who showed us around were so old!

And then suddenly spring came.

Spring in England is different — maybe you have to live through an English winter to understand it. The days lengthen, far more than they do in America, and the sky is bright, bright blue, not gray. The air feels soft and clean, you can smell damp earth and see leaves sparkling in the sun wherever you go.

It still rained, but there was sun every day.

When I opened my eyes one morning, there was even sun on my bed, and that was the day my mother and I went to look at the Brighton School for Girls. Brighton, my mother told me, was a seaside town. When we got off the train, the air was sparkling and smelled like salt; and at the school — which was a very short walk from the sea — all the windows and the white front door sparkled in the sun.

It looked like a clean, happy place. A comfortable-looking lady in a tweed skirt and two sweaters — one cardigan, one pullover — showed us around.

I liked it all until she opened the door of a dormitory. The beds were covered with thin, pale green bedspreads (exactly the same pale green as the desks at St. Vincent's) and pinned to each pillow was a small piece of lined white paper (not cut out with scissors, but ripped by hand — neatly, but still ripped) with a girl's name on it. All the names were in the same handwriting.

I took my mother's hand and held it tightly; she looked down at me, a little surprised (I don't usually hold her hand).

"What's the matter?" she said, as soon as we were back on the sidewalk.

"It's the best one we've seen so far, but . . . I don't like it." I didn't like those pale bedspreads and little ripped pieces of paper, but that wasn't a real reason. "There's just something about it that isn't quite right."

Then I thought of one good reason, something that would make sense to her.

"And it's not in the country, though it's nice that it's by the ocean."

My mother smiled, but it was a tired smile, I thought.

"Maybe Daddy will find something!" I said.

"Maybe he will," she said, and *that* smile looked happy.

I was right. One night he came home and said he'd found the perfect school.

"I drove down to Kent after lunch, and as soon as I saw Sibton

Park, I knew it was the one," he said, more to my mother than to me; then he laughed a little, almost as though he was embarrassed. "I fell in love with it." He handed me a small, thin booklet. " 'Ere 'ave a butcher's at this!"

The grown-up code — the rhyming slang! Have a butcher's hook (look) at this.

The booklet showed a big, rosy-brick building surrounded by fields. SIBTON PARK it said in blue letters. It sounded like a Jane Austen novel.

Inside were pictures of meadows with horses, and girls riding, and girls in the stable petting a horse (it was in a loose box, with bars at the top, exactly like the ones in the happy part of *Black Beauty*), and girls in their pajamas on their beds,

Sibton Park

The brochure cover.

Inside it said:

Sibton Park is a beautiful Queen Anne house standing in its own grounds of 88 acres…the foundations of the house go back to the reign of Edward III.… Each girl is encouraged to explore her own potential and to take pleasure in the success of others as well as her own. We believe in the old-fashioned value that consideration for other people is at the root of good manners.… Children whose parents are abroad may spend all or part of the holidays at school. It is Mrs. Ridley-Day's home and the school is never closed.

A picture from inside the brochure.

talking. It looked better than the boarding schools in the books: older, more strange and magical, more like the house in *The Secret Garden* than a school. There was a little map of the school and grounds, and there were gardens all over: a rose garden, a Tudor garden (what was that?). Meanwhile my father was excitedly telling my mother about the headmistress, and how old the house was (some parts were almost seven hundred years old, he said); I didn't really listen until his voice changed. By the change, I could tell something was wrong.

"Term starts the day after tomorrow," he said.

"But she'll need lots of new clothes, and I'll have to sew name tapes on everything — couldn't she go a day or two later?"

He shook his head. "They won't take children once the term has started. I have the clothes list right here," he said quickly, eagerly. She didn't say anything, and he went on: "Mrs. Ridley-Day said you can get all the uniform things at Peter Jones, and that they can send whatever she won't need right away straight to the school."

He pulled a piece of paper out of his pocket and my mother and I both looked at it.

"Jodhpurs, a RIDING jacket!" I said. "Oh, Daddy! Can I take it to show Emmy?"

"I signed you up for ballet, too," he called after me; as I ran out I heard him talking excitedly and my mother sort of laughing and saying, "Honestly, Art!"

My mother and I went shopping right after breakfast. First, she ordered name tapes (a long strip of white material with your name on it over and over in little capital letters: you could choose the color of the letters and I chose blue), and the man PROMISED that they would be ready by the end of the day. These had to be sewn inside all my clothes, even the socks, my mother said. She was worried about getting it done on time.

"I'm such a slow seamstress."

I had to try on a lot of clothes. The only interesting ones were the string gloves for riding — they really did look and feel like they were made out of string! Maybe they were! They

This is the list, with my mother's notes and check marks. Walking shoes laced up and had thick soles. House shoes were like Mary Janes, only made of brown leather. The shorts were culottes: they were made out of wool. "Fawn" was a sort of warm beige color. "Knickers" were brown and a little bigger and heavier than underpants. You wore them OVER your underpants (why you needed them I never knew). "Vests" were undershirts.

didn't have the jodhpurs and tweed jacket in my size. The man who measured me seemed surprised that I was going away to school, and when my mother said I was eight he said, "She's a bit small for her age, isn't she?"

It was true. I kept hoping that someday I would get taller; both of my parents are tall, and Emmy was tall for her age, too. In fact, by this time we were about the same height. But, so far I hadn't grown.

My mother and Jill started sewing on the name tapes as soon as we got home — my mother's stitches were tiny and perfectly even. As soon as things were done my mother checked them off on her list and put them in a trunk.

There was also a small brown suitcase called an "overnight case." She packed a dressing gown like the ones the girls in the books had and pajamas and a "sponge bag" — that was a pink plastic bag filled with soap, a washcloth, shampoo, a toothbrush, toothpaste, and a brush and comb. She said I could put the rest of the things of mine that I wanted to bring in this case myself, and that I could choose what to take.

I didn't bring the dolls — in the stories no one had dolls and it wouldn't be any fun to play with them without Emmy anyway. I chose *Pride and Prejudice* (the book about the five sisters; my parents had given me my own copy for Christmas), *Little Women, Melissa Ann* (a book about an orphan), and a fat blue book called *Blackie's Schoolgirl's Omnibus* that had three novels about boarding school in it. I wrote my name and our address in America in each book. I packed the card with Henry's address on it and all his letters inside the books so they wouldn't get ripped. I was going to leave the fortune-catcher at home, but then I unfolded it and put it in, too, very carefully. And I put in the diary and pen I had gotten for Christmas — I'd only written in the diary once, but maybe at the school I would want to. I put in an ink bottle, too, but my mother took that out.

"But then how can I write?" I said.

"They'll have ink at the school," she said quietly, without looking up from the ink bottle in her hand.

When she did look at me, I thought she looked a little sad, but then she smiled and said, "You'll have a lot to write about, and you can write letters to all of us to tell us what it's like: I'm putting in lots of envelopes and stamps. Daddy and I will write to you, of course, and Emmy, too — it will be good practice for her — and Willy and Bubby can draw pictures."

When I woke up the next day, the day I was leaving for boarding school, it was very sunny.

"Emmy! Are you awake?"

She didn't answer, so I got out of my bed and went over to hers. She sat up slowly and sleepily.

"I want to ask you something very important," I said. "Guard my dolls. Don't let Willy and Bubby play with them. You can check on them, but we'll still have the rule about not working each others'. Okay?" She nodded. "Promise?"

"I promise."

"Good."

The dolls said good-bye to each other, and then I put all mine in their own beds, under the covers, and put the beds inside the white chest.

It was a school day for Emmy and Willy, and Jill was taking Bubby with them, too, because by the time she came home, my parents and I would be at the train station. I followed them all to the front door. Willy and Bubby kissed me good-bye, and I kissed them back and gave them each a hug.

Emmy and I looked at each other, and then she started to cry.

"Emmy, don't cry!" I said. "Please don't cry! It's not very long until May sixteenth!"

(That was the first day they would be allowed to visit me, and of course they would come.)

"That's right, buck up!" Jill said.

We both ignored her.

"But it won't be the same — it won't be the same ever again," Emmy said, still crying.

I thought that was probably true; but I didn't say so. I said, "Think of your pet bird!"

My parents had promised to get her a budgerigar — a small parrot people in England have as a pet — as a sort of consolation present for me going away.

Then I made our "I hate this" face (the one I always made before I walked upstairs to my London classroom) and Emmy sort of smiled and made hers back at me, and then they left. . . . I stood in the doorway, and after a few steps, Emmy stopped. She turned around, with her hands still in her pockets, and we looked at each other one last time, and then I waved and ran into the house.

I went downstairs: our room was still sunny and very quiet and white. It felt a little funny to be in there without Emmy and Willy and Bubby. . . . by the time they were home again, I'd be gone. The room was so white, so still!

Emmy, exactly the way she was dressed and standing when she stopped and looked back at me (though this picture was taken a few weeks later).

When it was time for us to leave, my mother buttoned me into my new gray wool

coat (with a name tape neatly stitched into the inside collar with tiny tight stitches, all exactly alike), and a straw hat with a red ribbon round the brim — part of the new uniform. That had a nametape sewn into it, too.

No one took pictures that day (this was taken several weeks later), but this is the hat I was wearing.

My father was wearing a tweed jacket and my mother wore her pretty pink suit.

We took a taxi to Charing Cross, the train station. They weren't coming to the school —

they were just putting me on the "reserved car" (my mother said that meant a whole carriage just for girls going to Sibton Park).

But when we got to the platform we didn't see any car marked "Sibton Park," or any other girls. My father told my mother and me to wait while he went to find out what was happening. When he came back, he looked very embarrassed (I don't think I'd ever seen him embarrassed before) and told us that he'd called the school: all the other girls had already gone on an earlier train; someone would meet this one.

"The same mistake was made about her," he said.

A very big girl wearing a gray coat and straw hat just like mine was standing a few feet away, scowling awkwardly. Her name was Lindsey Cohen, and my father said we could take the train to Sibton Park together. Lindsey Cohen got on, and then my father said to give him a kiss, it was time to go.

"So long! See you May sixteenth!" he said, and looked at my mother.

She bent down and hugged me; I held her neck very tightly for a minute. I could smell her Arpège perfume; then she kissed me and I let go. When she stood up, her lips and chin were trembling. She smiled, with her mouth wobbling a little.

I got on the train and sat down next to the window, across from Lindsey Cohen; my parents both waved to me and I waved back. The train started with a jerk and noise — a whistle, and then that horrible clacking that keeps getting faster. We all kept waving.

I kept thinking: I cannot cry, I *will not cry*, especially in front of Lindsey Cohen.

On the wall just above her head was a small glass box with a sign below it saying:

TO STOP THE TRAIN

IN CASES OF EMERGENCY,

PULL DOWN THE CHAIN.

PENALTY FOR IMPROPER USE, £5.

I wondered what would happen if I pulled the chain: How would it stop the train? Of course, I wouldn't pull it — this wasn't an emergency. And I wouldn't cry. After all, I *wanted* to go to boarding school.

"Make sure you're right, then go ahead," Davy Crockett said, and he did, even at the Alamo. That was much worse than this!

I would NOT cry. And if it felt like I might, I could go into the little hallway and look out the window there, keeping my back to the compartment.

Chapter Fourteen: Sibton Park

I didn't cry, but I did walk into the little hallway. I pressed my face to the window and looked hard. Once we got into the real country, there were fields, deep green and (often) full of sheep. When I went back into the compartment, I fell asleep. I woke up a little in the taxi but I didn't REALLY wake up until I was sitting at a long wood table late that night, eating cold roast beef. It was rare (just how I like it), and as I ate, I got more awake. Lindsey Cohen was sitting next to me, and we were at Sibton Park.

The room was big and bare, with three long wooden tables (all empty), squares of gray stone for a floor, and lots of big windows (it was too dark outside to see anything out of them). It was also a little bit cold.

A grown-up came in and said she'd bring me to my dormitory. She led me through a long passage with

Sibton Park, as it looks when you come in the front gates and go a little way down the front drive. The house had been added onto over the years, and each side of it (there were more than four) looked quite different. The front was the most formal.

coathooks and kids' raincoats all along the walls, and a brick floor so old that the center dipped down from all those feet over the years.

We went up steep stairs and through a wider, fancier hallway with wood floors, then up more stairs into a small room with no furniture in it, and down two steps into a long, straight, wide, white hall with lots of closed doors.

The first door on the right had a white wooden sign with neat black letters saying: WELLINGTON. The next said: WATERLOO. Then, above a little step on the left, the door said: WC.

She opened the door, and I saw a little white room with just a toilet, no sink or bathtub. I stepped up into it and closed the door.

When I came out, we walked past more doors and stopped at NELSON. This, she whispered, was my dormitory, and I'd need to get

A dormitory at Sibton Park — not Nelson.

ready for bed quietly so I didn't wake "the others." Then she opened the door.

The room was big, with tall, old-fashioned windows open (a breeze and a silvery gray light came through them, and outside I could see a leafy branch), a fireplace, and five beds: four with girls in them, one empty. There was a little sink in the corner; she pointed to it and watched me wash and get into bed, then whispered good-night.

As soon as she was gone, all the girls sat up in their beds. One by one, they said hello and whispered their names, very politely: Rosemary Hitchcock, Sarah Riley, Catherine Marshall, and Hazel Fogarty. They seemed nice (only Sarah Riley had kind of a snobbish voice, I thought).

"My name is Elizabeth Koponen," I said, "but everyone calls me Libby."

"Are you American?" Catherine Marshall said. She was in a bed by itself across from the door. My bed was in the middle of a row of three beds against a wall.

"Yes," I said proudly. I *am* proud of being an American. "Don't ever give me tea — if you do, I'll have to pour it out on the floor, in honor of the Boston Tea Party."

"What's that?"

I told them about the grown-ups in Boston dressing up like Indians in the middle of the night and dumping all the tea from the English ships into the Boston harbor. There was a little pause when I was done, and then Catherine Marshall said, "That's interesting."

There was another little pause, and then Hazel Fogarty asked if I'd ever been "away at school" before, and I said no, and they started telling me all about Sibton Park.

"Your first term you'll be teased — new girls always are."

I asked how long you were a new girl, and they said for your first term, but that you weren't an old girl until you'd been there a year.

They'd been there for three or four years: they were all older than I was. I asked about the headmistress, Mrs. Ridley-Day. My father had talked about her a lot — he'd said she was beautiful and "a real lady," and that he'd chosen the school because of what she was like. I didn't say that; I just asked the girls if they liked Mrs. Ridley-Day.

"Call her Marza. We all do. It's Greek for 'mother,'" Catherine Marshall said.

"Does she have a husband?"

"He's dead — he died in the war."

"That's when she started the school."

"The house is hers," Sarah said.

We talked on and on — I didn't feel sleepy at all and I don't think anyone else did, either. After a while we stopped whispering and talked out loud. There was a rule against talking after Lights Out, they said, but no one ever obeyed it and people were always getting punished for it.

Catherine said, "One night the whole school was talking — except for Alice and Tina, they're prefects and the oldest girls in the school —"

"— and the next morning at prayers Marza said there would be no sweets that day!" Hazel said.

I knew that "sweets" meant candy.

"Do you usually have sweets?"

"Yes, every day after dinner we line up and can choose two each."

"What kind?"

"Toffees, or acid drop spangles, or peppermints, or boiled sweets. On Sunday we always have Cadbury's."

That wasn't in any of the books. But they seemed to like school as much as the girls in the books did.

We talked on and on. I told them that on the train, Lindsey Cohen had hardly talked to me at all, and Catherine said, "She doesn't like Americans — her father married one and she can't bear her step-mother. I shouldn't worry."

I asked where the horses were, and if they could ride them whenever they wanted, and everyone started talking at once, and Hazel Fogarty (they called her "Foggy") was jumping up and down on her bed, imitating someone who couldn't ride, and we were all laughing when the door opened.

All the noise stopped and everyone quickly got under the covers. A lady stood tall and straight in the doorway, like a queen. She had gray hair in one long, thick braid that curved over the front collar of her dressing gown. I could see her quite well in the light from the hall and I knew who she was: Mrs. Ridley-Day. She *was* very beautiful.

She didn't say anything, just looked. Everyone was lying down, breathing quietly and slowly. Then . . .

"Catherine Marshall, were you talking?"

No answer.

"Hazel Fogarty, were you talking?"

No answer.

"Sarah Riley, were you talking?"

No answer.

"Elizabeth Koponen, were you talking?"

"Yes, Marza," I said proudly—(in books, the girls always owned up).

There was a little pause and then she said, in a different voice, "You're far too young for this wing of the house."

She didn't say anything else, but even after she left, there was no more talking — except that Catherine Marshall whispered, "When she asks, you don't have to answer."

I think they all went to sleep after that. I didn't — I lay on my back with my eyes open, thinking and listening. The girls were nice . . . they liked me . . . Sibton Park wouldn't be like St. Vincent's. . . .

The night was very quiet — so quiet that I could hear leaves rustling outside the window.

After a while I heard a sound I hadn't heard in a long time, a sound that felt safe and familiar even before I knew what it was: a car far away coming closer and closer, getting louder and louder, until its lights swept the room fast. Then the room got dark again, and slowly, the sound faded away.

I heard that every night in my room in America.

I lay on my back, listening for the next one. Finally I heard it. First the engine from far away getting closer and louder — it felt lonely and adventurous from far away, but safe, too; and then exciting when the sound was really loud and the lights swept the room. Then the sound went farther and farther away until I couldn't hear it anymore, and the night was still and peaceful and quiet; until the next safe sound — a car from far away coming closer.

Chapter Fifteen:
Talking to a Real Horse

The next day, there weren't any classes: The first day of term was always a day just for everyone to get settled in.

As soon as I was by myself and could, I thought, do what I wanted (which was after I'd been moved into my new dormitory, the Night Nursery, and been shown around the school), I ran to the big meadow where the horses were.

I was a little surprised by how BIG they were and decided not to get too close. There was a dead tree, gray and smooth like driftwood, lying on its side in the sun, and I stood near that, watching the horses eating grass. After a while a big gray one lifted its head up and looked at me.

It walked towards me slowly, kind of curiously, with its neck stretched out, swishing its tail. It looked very relaxed. It came right up to me and sniffed me. Then it touched me — sort of nudged me — with its nose. I didn't know what to do. In books they always

A pony in the big meadow. I took this picture myself, with a Brownie camera my father had given me.

said horses could tell if you were scared, and that quick movements frightened them, so I just stood very still and tried not to be afraid. The horse bent down its head and shoved me with its nose until I was pushed back against the dead tree, and it was standing right in front of me. This wasn't done in a MEAN way — it was as though the horse was old and bossy, and saying, "Get over there."

So I did.

Then I was trapped between the horse and the tree. The horse's neck was higher than my head. I stood still and started talking to the horse in a quiet, steady voice, the way people did in books. The horse pushed its nose against my chest — hard — so my back pressed into the tree, and then, very slowly, it rubbed its whole face against me, pushing hard, rubbing up and down my chest and stomach. It closed its eyes and rubbed the space in between them, and then the long bony part of its face that went from between its eyes down to its nose — over and over, up and down my body — and then it turned its head and put one foot out in front of the others (even its feet were big) and rubbed one side of its face against me, then the other.

It didn't hurt, except where a bump on the tree was pressing into my back. I kept talking, quietly and calmly. Finally the horse kind of shook itself all over (as though it was saying, "Oh! I needed that!"); gave me one last nudge with its nose; and ambled away, head hanging down, neck stretched out, tail swishing. It stopped a few feet away from me and started munching grass again.

That was the first time I ever talked to a horse.

I felt a little proud of myself and very happy. I had talked to a real horse. The books had been right (I like it when things in books turn out to be true) — I'd remembered what they said to do and I'd done it.

When something frightening happens, the best thing to do, I think, is to stay calm, figure out what to do, and then (even if you're afraid) make yourself do it, no matter what. "Make sure you're right, then go ahead," as Davy Crockett said.

Anyway, although it was a little scary at first, it was neat to have been that close to a real horse.

I walked back to the house slowly, out of the meadow and into "the paddock" and up some brick steps. Then I was on a big smooth lawn called the Lower Garden, with bushes cut into fancy shapes. The part of the house I could see from here (the house was huge, with more than a hundred rooms) was made of

The paddock steps, with the Lower Garden and part of the house in the background.

rose-colored brick; it even looked old. (I knew from the little booklet that it had been built in 1300-something.)

And what I could see was only part of Sibton Park — there was another huge lawn called the Upper Garden, a Tudor Garden (twisty

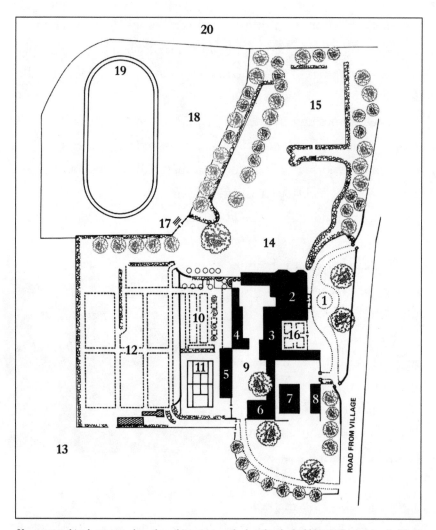

You can use this plan to see where these things were and what they looked like. **1.** *Front drive* **2.** *Main house (Marza)* **3.** *Classrooms on ground floor, Night Nursery and other junior dormitories on second* **4.** *More classrooms (French)* **5.** *Art room—later, theater for play* **6.** *Classrooms* **7.** *Stables* **8.** *Laundry* **9.** *Yard* **10.** *Rose Garden* **11.** *Tennis courts* **12.** *Kitchen Garden* **13.** *Meadows and fields* **14.** *Lower Garden* **15.** *Upper Garden* **16.** *Tudor Garden* **17.** *Steps up to lawn* **18.** *Paddock* **19.** *Ring* **20.** *Out of bounds*

More of the Lower Garden, with different angles of the house in the background.

little brick paths arranged in a complicated pattern around little hedges, with an old sundial in the middle), tennis courts, and the Rose Garden. Our whole yard in America could have fit into half the Rose Garden. It was strange to think that one person owned all of it, that it used to be her house.

I opened a dark green door in a brick wall and then I knew where I was again — right next to our part of the house. I ran up to the big room called the Nursery.

Matron was sitting at a round wooden table, folding clothes. She was sixteen-and-a-half, but she seemed older than our baby-sitters in America — she seemed like a grown-up, not a teenager, maybe because she was so big. She was almost as tall as my father and I think even bigger.

Everyone called her "Matron," but (as I found out later — I didn't remember any Matrons in the school stories) it wasn't her name: it was her job. I don't know what she did while we were having lessons, but when we weren't, she was usually in the Nursery, or someplace else where we could easily find her

The matron at English boarding schools for younger children looks after the girls somewhat the way a nanny does and is called "Matron," just as nannies are called "Nanny." The Matron my first term was unusually young, interested in us, and fun.

and talk to her. She also put us to bed, gave us our baths, and looked after us when we were ill.

Everything about her was round: she had a round face and shiny blonde hair in a round bun at the back, very fair skin, and round navy-blue eyes. That day she was wearing a navy-blue dress with a white collar and white rims on the sleeves. This was her first term at Sibton Park, too; she had just left school herself and was only going to be at Sibton Park for one term — she would be going to the university in September. She wanted to be a writer, too. She had told me all this after breakfast, when she was moving me into my new dormitory and showing me around. I liked her.

When I came in from the meadow, she said, "My goodness, Libby, look at your jumper! Whatever have you been doing?"

I looked. My sweater ("jumper") and culottes and even my socks were covered with horse hairs. I told her what had happened.

"That must have been Nella. A big gray mare?"

"I don't know if it was a mare or not — it was big, and seemed old."

"She is. Twenty at least."

I was pleased that I'd guessed right about the age and decided it would be all right to ask a question.

"Why do you think she did that?"

"Scratching herself."

She explained that horses' faces get very itchy and that they can't scratch themselves or each other, and that a person in wool clothes is the very best thing.

"For their backs they roll on the grass," Brioney (the seven-year-old in my new dormitory) said — she was lolling on a bed by the window. "Like this!"

She rolled on the bed, rubbing her back into it, and waved her arms and legs. Her feet were big — although she was younger, Brioney was much bigger than I was. She had big bones and big round eyes that were so blue they sometimes looked green, and strong bones in her cheeks — even her mouth was big. That might make her sound ugly but she wasn't — later one of the seniors said Brioney would grow up to be "a beauty." She was kind of babyish, though.

While Brioney was rolling around like a horse itching its back, Clare came to the door. She was in my new dormitory, too, and she was my age. She was a new girl as well. Her last name was Sweeting and she seemed sweet, but I liked her. She had blonde hair and very fair skin; everything about her was light — even her voice.

She came into the room quietly, and then she asked me, kind of shyly, if I would like to go for a walk with her.

"Sure!" I said.

Brioney sat up eagerly, as though she wanted to go too, but Matron said, "Stay here with me, Brioney — you can help butter the bread."

So Clare and I went by ourselves. We were wearing exactly the same clothes: fawn-colored jumpers (we each had on a pullover with a cardigan over it), gray wool culottes, and fawn-colored knee socks. Only our shoes were different. Having a uniform was kind of fun, I thought.

She told me that she had an older sister named Carol who had been at Sibton for two years. I didn't say anything, and there was a little pause.

Then she asked me what my "hobbies" were.

"What do you mean?" I said. I thought of the school stories. "Things like stamp collecting?"

"Well, yes. Things you're interested in — that you do just for the fun of it."

Playing isn't really a hobby.

"Does writing stories count as a hobby?" I said.

"Yes, of course," she said.

"Well, then: writing. I do write, quite a lot — I'm going to be an author when I grow up." Clare looked interested, and asked more questions. I told her one of the Crazy Old Witch stories, and when the Witch said "My foot!" she laughed. Talking about my writing felt strange, but fun, and after that we talked about lots of other things. We walked around the fields talking until Brioney came out and said it was time for dinner.

Chapter Sixteen:
Manners and Matron

All three of us walked to the Dining Hall together, and when we got there, Matron told me that I would be sitting next to her at meals, so she could teach me to "eat properly."

That, I learned over the next few days, meant always holding your fork in your left hand, and your knife in your right, and eating from the back of the fork, instead of the front. You used the knife to push food onto the back of the fork. It was hard, especially with peas, which we had a lot — they were always sliding off the fork, and of course, you couldn't use your fingers to push them back on.

There were lots of other eating rules, too, that we don't have in America: When you butter bread, put the butter on your plate; then (with your butter knife, not a regular knife) put a little bit — just what you're going to eat at that bite, no more — on the bread, eat it, then, when you're going to take another bite, put on a little more. NEVER butter the whole piece, never scrape your knife on the side of the plate.

This is what I mean by the back of the fork.

When you're finished, put your knife and fork together in the middle of the plate, with the fork's prongs facing up. When you're not finished, put the handle of the knife on the right side of the plate, with the blade in the middle, and the fork handle on the left side of the plate, with the prongs in the middle and facing down. This is so the servants know when to take your plate away and when not to.

Not done.   Done.

There are rules not just for how you eat, but what you talk about at meals.

One day my milk had yellowy splotches floating in it.

"Yuck!" I said. Matron looked cross. "Yuck!" wasn't an English word, I knew that, but I was so surprised by the milk that it slipped out. I held out my cup: "Look!"

She looked.

"You're jolly lucky — you got the cream!"

She frowned at me — then she frowned at Brioney and some other people, who were giggling. They stopped.

I took a sip before she could tell me to, but I could feel the lumps in it, and I made a face.

Matron looked even more annoyed.

There was a little pause and then she said, in her storytelling voice, "Once, there was a very important person."

Everyone put down their knives and forks (in the still-eating position) to listen — we loved it when Matron told stories.

"This very important person went to a luncheon party, and there was a caterpillar in his salad. So he folded it up in a piece of lettuce —," she imitated him putting the caterpillar in the middle of the lettuce, folding the lettuce neatly around it with his knife, and then pushing it firmly onto his fork, "— and ate it."

She imitated him chewing and swallowing politely, with no expression at all on his face.

The others were listening calmly; I was horrified.

"But WHY?" I said. "Why would he do that?"

I looked around — Clare was looking amused; she didn't laugh or smile, but I could tell something was making her laugh inside (you can tell by her eyes, and the corners of her mouth — they quiver a little). Matron looked at me and blinked in that mild, calm English way (it's how they show that they're surprised).

"He had to. He was a very important person."

The others nodded and went on eating, as though that made sense. It didn't to me. But I did understand that you don't make comments (or even a face) about food, no matter what. So that night, when we had the English idea of spaghetti — plates of plain spaghetti, which they called "macaroni," and a small pitcher of completely smooth, very runny ketchup to pour on top — I didn't say anything.

Chapter Seventeen:
Lessons

But I did still talk like myself during lessons.

Lessons started after quite a lot of others things had happened: When the bell first rang, we got up, dressed quickly, folded our mattresses in half (this was supposed to air them out), and went down to breakfast. Then we came back upstairs, made our beds, and lined up for prayers.

We marched through Marza's part of the house to a beautiful room called the Long Room. It had big fireplaces at both ends and dark wood square panels on all the walls. We stood in rows. Marza stood in front of us, next to a very polished little table, and the mistresses all stood on one side.

We bowed our heads and said a prayer, and then, when Marza picked up her hymn book, we opened ours. (The hymn number for the day was always written on a little board in our part of the house, where we lined up.)

Then Miss Day played the piano and we all sang. That morning it was one of our favorites, "Onward Christian Soldiers." We almost shouted the chorus:

Onward Christian SOLDiers!
Marching as to WAR!
With the cross of JEsus
Going on before!

The music to "Onward Christian Soldiers."

I liked singing that.

After the hymn, Marza made announcements, if there were any. Announcements were usually just which dorms had been talking after Lights Out and how they would be punished. But that morning she said that seniors could audition for the school play that day after lessons.

Then, slowly and majestically, she picked up her prayer book and hymn book and walked out, her back very straight. Then (this happened every day), Miss Day played "The British Grenadiers" and we marched out, row by row, and went to our form rooms for lessons.

Our form, IIB, was in a long, low, white metal building by itself. There were windows all along one side of it and all day sun poured in — sometimes, it even got hot.

Everyone in the class was younger than I was. They were all-day girls (girls who didn't sleep at the school but just came for lessons) except for Brioney and me and the only boy in the school, Mo.

Lessons were interesting — not at all like school in America. We read real books and copied *Alice in Wonderland* to practice our hand-writing, and out loud we read real poetry. We had English History, World History, and Ancient History. In Nature Study we found plants in the woods and fields and drew pictures of them. In Geography we copied maps and colored in the sea with short strokes of light blue pencils. For Singing we went to a special room and Miss Barton played the piano while we sang old folk songs like "My Bonnie Lies Over the Ocean" (after the first letter from Henry came, everyone thought it was hilarious to sing "My *Henry* lies over the ocean," nudging each other and looking at me) and "Loch Lomond."

I tried hard to be good at everything except singing: I have a terrible voice and I know it. (On my reports I always got "Poor." Once she added: "Shows some improvement, though.") French was hard, because I'd never had it. All the other kids had; and it was because I didn't know it that I was in IIB, not IIA with Clare and the other girls my age. So I tried extra hard at French.

That day, while everyone was coming in and getting settled, I said eagerly, "Who's going to be the star of the play?"

Miss Davenport gave me a scornful look.

"This isn't a Hollywood production, Libby," she said. "There is no *star*."

Then she told us what chapter to read. The first lesson each day was Scripture. We always read the chapter, then closed our Bibles and wrote down everything we could remember; she corrected our Scripture while we did our arithmetic.

Next, we had Composition, and that day she told us to write about something interesting that had happened over the holidays. I know that you're not supposed to complain and that no one in England does — I hadn't the night before about the spaghetti — but sometimes I just can't help it. I HATE writing about stupid subjects and I said so.

After a while, Miss Davenport said, "That will do, Libby," and told us to begin.

Everyone else started writing and I just sat there, glaring out the window. Miss Davenport ignored me. Finally, when there were only a few minutes left, I thought of the train trip to the school. I'd spent part of it standing outside the compartment, looking out the window until a man started talking to me. I decided to write about our conversation.

When she'd read all the compositions, Miss Davenport said mine was "hilarious — I laughed and laughed" (she had, I'd seen her), and then she said she would read it out loud to everyone else.

"Libby, you may stand outside while I read it."

I would have liked to stay and see what everyone thought (I'd be able to tell by their faces), but English people never act proud of what they've done; they always look embarrassed when people praise them. So I went outside.

Later, when we were playing by ourselves (we were allowed to play outside after lessons, and the two of us had climbed a tree), I asked Brioney what she thought of my composition. She said, "I didn't see what was so funny about it, except when you called the corridor 'the hall.'"

I hadn't meant it to be funny, so that was kind of a relief. Then we started talking about something else, and Clare and Mo climbed into the tree with us and we were all talking and playing when some seniors came by and somehow — I forget whose idea it was — we decided to have a competition to see who could hang from a branch the longest.

Clare, Mo, Brioney, and I were the competitors; Retina (Brioney's older sister) and Carol (Clare's older sister) and some other seniors were the audience. The rules were simple: Hang from the branch with just your hands. The branch was higher than any of us could reach from the ground, so we climbed out to it; the seniors (who were a lot taller than we were — they all always seemed huge to me) said they would lift us down when we were tired.

"Just say," Carol said, "and one of us will lift you down."

We grasped the branch with our hands (I clasped my fingers together; I couldn't see how the others were doing it) and dropped. It was a funny feeling, to be hanging from a branch with your feet high above the ground.

The seniors leaned against the fence to watch; Catherine Marshall was there and I think she wanted me to win. I wanted to win, too, of course; in fact, I REALLY wanted to. I thought I probably would: I was still very strong, probably stronger than any of them.

But after a while, my hands got a little sweaty and they started to slide apart. Clare and Brioney had already been lifted down: It was just Mo and me. I thought I could hang on if I just gripped tighter: My muscles weren't tired at all. Suddenly — before I could say anything at all — my hands slid completely apart and I fell.

Chapter Eighteen:
Mo, Brioney, and Tuppence

I landed right on my face. My tooth went through the skin just under my lip — I could feel the tooth do that, and blood trickling down, but the worst part was that I couldn't breathe at first. It's a sickening feeling: Has it ever happened to you? You can't breathe — it's as though there isn't any air in your lungs.

"Brioney, get Matron," Retina said.

As soon as I could talk, I said, "I'm okay," and sat up.

"Better not move until Matron has a look at you," Catherine Marshall said, but just as she said that, Matron came running up.

"I'm okay," I said again.

When we were walking back to the house by ourselves, I told her about not being able to breathe and how much it had scared me.

"You had the wind knocked out of you, that's all," she said in a definite, very reassuring voice. "Still, I think you'd better have the doctor about that lip."

The doctor came and stitched it up (he said I would have a little scar but because it was just under the lip it wouldn't show much), and to stay in bed for two days.

Being sick at Sibton Park was kind of fun: Matron put a big jug of lemonade next to my bed, so I could have a drink whenever I wanted to, and whenever she had time, she came in and read to me or told me stories. Sometimes she asked me to read her *my* stories, and I did. Sometimes she brought her sewing in and we just talked, and I liked that best of all.

While I was in bed by myself, I thought about the children at Sibton Park. I thought that they all looked very English and that I didn't, because of my slanted eyes — their eyes were so round. A lot of them had turned-up noses, and I wished I did, too.

Mo looked different from everyone else, too. It wasn't just that he was the only boy: He came from Persia. He always wore gray shorts, gray socks, a white shirt with a tie, and a gray pullover with a V-neck. He had a serious little face with a big, big nose and round dark eyes that often had a worried expression. He was the shortest boarder and I was the second shortest. The only people who ever played with him were Brioney and I.

He spoke English perfectly, with a perfect English accent, though he had a SLIGHT lisp (that means he couldn't quite say his s's), but some English children did, too — one senior said her r's like w's even though she was much older. We called him Mo, but his real name was Mohammed.

While I was sick, and she was sewing by my bed, I asked Matron why Mo was at Sibton Park, and she said, "The boys' schools won't take them until they're seven."

Mo was six. He had been at Sibton Park since he was four.

On my first day out of bed Mo and I went into the cow pasture together. First, we stood at the fence around the cricket field and watched the men playing. That wasn't very interesting.

Then we just walked around, talking — it was a perfect summer day with rich, clean English light and a few solid, puffy clouds making shadows on the grass. We had to watch the grass carefully because of the cow pats — they're completely flat and when they dry, they get hard. But I didn't want to step on a wet one.

"I wish I had a turned-up nose," I said.

I had practiced what this would look like in the looking glass (it's bad English to say "mirror") while I was in bed, and I showed him. I put one finger on the skin between my nostrils and pushed so my nose turned up.

"Like this."

He looked at me, seriously, obviously thinking about it.

"I think you look really ugly like that," he said.

I was surprised, but pleased, too. The way he said it sounded like I didn't look ugly when I didn't do it. I could tell he really meant it.

There was a cow lying down near us — a big fat one, white with brown splotches. We stood next to her and she didn't move — she just let us stare at her.

"Have you ever ridden a cow?" Mo said.

"No, have you?"

"Watch."

He walked even closer to the cow and I followed: Her back wasn't flat like a horse's. It had a big bone sticking out in a tall ridge that sloped down to her fat sides. He put his hands on her backbone and stretched one leg up, but when he tried to put it over the cow, she stood up and walked away. We followed her: As soon as she lay down, he tried to get on again, but she always stood up before he could do it.

"Let's try to ride one of the horses," I said.

So we climbed the fence into the horse meadow. We were trying to sneak up on a Shetland pony named Frisky when Brioney came running out. She's a pretty good rider (I watched the riding lessons but couldn't ride because my riding clothes weren't ready yet).

Brioney said that Tuppence would be the best horse for us. "Miss Monkman always puts beginners on him."

I thought Frisky or one of the other Shetland ponies would be better, because they were smaller, but she said no, Tuppence was more "trusty." Mo didn't really want to ride a horse (he didn't take riding lessons), and I really did, so we decided that Brioney would hold Tuppence while Mo helped me get on. It wasn't hard to catch Tuppence: He didn't even stop eating grass when Brioney took hold of his halter.

I tried to grab his mane and swing myself up onto his back, the way cowboys do. But I couldn't.

"Give her a leg up, Mo," Brioney said. I held the mane tightly in my left hand while Mo held his hands together under my knee and I tried to swing my other leg over, but Tuppence kept stepping aside.

Then I held the mane with both hands and pulled up while

Brioney and Mo both pushed and boosted until my stomach was on Tuppence's back! I was on a horse!

I slithered around until my whole body was sprawled on his back, but before I could sit all the way up, he flung his back into the air. (Horses do this by kicking both their back legs up at the same time so high that their back goes up. This is called bucking.) I hung onto the mane; my body bounced up and down.

"Hang on! Get your leg over him!" Brioney shouted.

I tried — I held the mane tightly with both hands and tried to pull myself up, but before I could Tuppence bucked again — I bounced up into the air and his mane jerked out of my hands and then the ground hit my stomach, hard. (I know that really *I fell*, but it seemed that the ground flew up at me and hit my stomach. I've fallen off plenty of horses since then, and that's always how it feels; it was just more surprising the first time.)

Brioney and Mo bent over me. Mo's little round face looked even more worried than usual.

"I'm okay," I said when I could talk. "I just had the wind knocked out of me."

I sat up: I wasn't bleeding anyplace. Brioney said, "We'll help you get back on."

"Get back on? Are you mad?" said Mo.

"But Miss Monkman says you should always get right back on after you fall off, she always makes us."

"Don't be ridiculous."

All I could think while they argued (Mo won by just saying "NO" in a very firm voice) was: Finally, I'd ridden a real horse — not for very long, but I *had* ridden. And soon my riding clothes would come and I'd ride every day.

Mo slept in a room by himself. Brioney and I sometimes used to sneak in to talk to him after we'd all been put to bed. Once when we went in, he was crying: We couldn't see his face, but we could hear him and see his back shaking under the covers.

Brioney and Tuppence: I took this picture, but not on the day in this chapter. It is in the same meadow, though.

We stood in the doorway, waited a bit, and then I whispered, "Mo?"

"Leave me alone!" I didn't know what to do. "Go away!"

I thought that probably he didn't want us to see him crying. At Sibton Park (and in the school stories, too), people called crying "blubbing." No one did it much.

Brioney and I looked at each other again and then, without talking, went back to the Night Nursery and got in bed. I didn't blame Mo *at all* for crying. He was only six years old! He was the only boy! He had to sleep in a room all by himself; we had each other.

I wondered if other people were ever homesick. Sometimes when we were getting into our pajamas Brioney sat on her bed sobbing and shouting, "Ret! I want Ret!" and one of us would run upstairs and find her. Retina would put Brioney on her lap and cuddle her until she stopped crying. But she never said what she was crying about. Brioney was only seven: I didn't blame her, either.

But no one else "blubbed" — or if they did, they did it very privately. I never heard anyone use the word "homesick." It was one of the things you weren't supposed to talk about — or even feel, maybe. No one talked about missing her family, either — in fact, I was the only person in the whole school who ever talked about her family at all.

Chapter Nineteen:
Bubby and Bubbité

That started in French, which we had in a small, sunny room with a big round table.

We sat around that with Mademoiselle: She was tiny, the tiniest grown-up I'd ever known, with huge, round green-gray eyes, freckles, and lots of dark hair on top of her head in a big, but neat, knot. She wore her skirts very long: Whether this was because she was so small she couldn't find any that fit her properly, or whether she just liked them that way I don't know.

Maybe it was because she was so tiny, maybe it was because of her age (she was, we knew, only eighteen), but she didn't seem grown up to me. Matron was only sixteen, and she DID seem grown up — but then, she was big, very big.

Everyone always obeyed Matron; hardly anyone obeyed Mademoiselle — once, when people were being very naughty (we were all actually running around the table, laughing), she started to cry.

Then we sat down; I felt sorry. Mademoiselle was so little! Even her voice was little — little and high — and she didn't speak English very well.

I had French with Mo and the youngest children from IA: They were all-day girls and one of them was only FOUR! It was not very interesting, just lots of memorizing, until one day Mademoiselle (we pronounced it "Mamzelle") said she thought we were ready to read a storybook. We were very excited; at least, I was.

She brought out six books — one for each of us and one for her. They were all pale green with hard covers, not very thick, and called *Les Lapins*.

"Who knows what is Lapin?" Mademoiselle said. I opened the book: There were pictures of rabbits — a mother, a father, and two children, all wearing human clothes.

"The rabbits!" I said excitedly, and this was right.

She told us all to open our books, and then she read the first page of the story out loud — in French, of course — and we listened and followed along in our books.

The rabbits in the family were Monsieur Lapin, Madame Lapin, and their two children, Pierre and Bubbité (this was pronounced Boo-bee-tay).

Then, she asked who could translate the first sentence into English, and we all looked at the words — and the pictures.

"This is Mr. Lapin," I said. "And this is Mrs. Lapin."

Mamzelle said, "Bon, Libby! But what is Lapin?"

"Rabbit," I said. "Mr. and Mrs. Rabbit."

(I knew that, but I thought it sounded better in French — less babyish. But I wanted to get to the next page in the story, so I didn't argue.)

"Bon. Mo, the next sentence, please?"

Mo said, "They have two children, Pierre and Bubbité — Peter and . . . how shall I translate *Bubbité?*"

Mamzelle seemed to be thinking.

"Bubby!" I said.

Mamzelle looked at me, puzzled.

"My youngest sister's name is Bubby! Can we translate it into Bubby?"

One of the little girls said Bubby was a funny name, and Mo said, "I like the name Bubby."

I said, "It's not her real name. We call her Bubby because when she was a baby she had really chubby cheeks, and we — my sister Emmy and my brother Willy and I — used to put our fingers on her mouth —," I put my fingers at the corners of my mouth, "— and push them together, like this. While we did it we used to say 'Chub-a-bub-bub!' So we just started calling her Bubby."

(This was the kind of conversation Miss Davenport would never have allowed, but with Mamzelle, we could do pretty much whatever we wanted.)

Mamzelle — and everyone else — laughed; Mamzelle said in her excited French way, "Yes, yes, let's call her Bubby!"

We turned the page: It showed Madame Lapin cooking something. The Lapin family seemed to be very excitable — they were not at all English. Almost all of their conversation ended in exclamation points, no matter what they were talking about:

"But what is this? The saucepan is missing! Pierre! Pierre!
Where is the saucepan?" cries Madame Lapin.
"I do not know, Maman!"
"Monsieur Lapin! Where is the saucepan?"

French was better once we started reading this book; and it was fun to translate Bubbité as Bubby. At home, I never really THOUGHT very much about Willy and Bubby — they were just kind of there, round, chubby things who were always giggling — but at Sibton Park, I did. It was odd to think that now Bubby was three and I hadn't been there on her birthday, and of a family birthday party without me.

Chapter Twenty: Sunday

I knew they'd had a party because my mother told me about it in one of her letters. She wrote to me about twice a week, and I wrote to her every Sunday. After church, we all had to go to our form rooms and write letters to our parents; but I sometimes wrote letters at other times, too.

Everything about Sunday was different from all the other days. We had sausages instead of bacon for breakfast: one big fat English sausage each on a piece of fried bread (fried bread sounds awful, but it's delicious, especially with marmalade). Then we washed and put on our straw hats with the red ribbon, white gloves, and, if it was chilly, the gray wool uniform coats. We were already wearing our Sunday dresses.

We gathered in a big square hall with a stone floor, as usual. But this Sunday, the seniors stood on one side and the juniors stood at the other, so the seniors could pick their partners for church.

We had this new rule because the juniors fidgeted and whispered and giggled so much in church that Marza had decided that we (the juniors) had to be separated from each other.

So, we were each going to have a senior as a partner.

The partners would walk to church together and sit next to each other. The idea was that the senior would make the junior behave.

Sisters, Marza had said, could be partners. So Retina picked Brioney, and Carol picked Clare. The head girl, Alice, walked up to Veryan and nodded: Of course, she would pick Veryan — she was Veryan's favorite senior. At Sibton Park it was the custom for each senior (girl in the Upper School) to look after a junior (a girl in the Lower School) — not all the time, but when someone older was wanted. All the juniors who didn't have older sisters at the school had a senior who did this.

If, for example, Veryan was upset, we would go get Alice and she would come down to the Night Nursery and talk to Veryan. Matron, I guess, was the one who did this for me, though the only time she'd ever had to was the time I fell out of the tree. So I didn't know who would pick me.

Another prefect did: a girl called Buffer. She frowned and then nodded at me. I'd never talked to her before, but I knew who she was, and I stood on line next to her.

> In school stories, the prefects were in charge of things like making people go to bed on time; at Sibton Park, they were just older girls Marza picked to be prefects. There were four.

When everyone had a partner, we walked out of the school in what they called a "crocodile" (a line), two by two.

I knew that Buffer's real name was Elizabeth — since there were so many Elizabeths in the school they all had nicknames — but I don't know why her nickname was Buffer. She was tall, with gray eyes and brown hair cut straight across her forehead, like mine! Only her hair was much thicker and much neater. She was a lot bigger than I was, but most of the seniors were.

Even though Buffer took long steps, she was kind of a slow walker, and I walked a little in front of her, turning around or walking backward to look up at her.

She seemed very serious. She didn't talk much on the way to church; I did. I think I talked the whole way without stopping. Every now and then she'd give a sudden laugh and then (just as suddenly) her face would get serious again.

I always liked the walk to church: It was along lanes with wide strips of grass on each side — that rich English grass that feels springy under your feet. I don't really remember what I talked about — whatever I was thinking or noticing, probably; I didn't really pay much attention to what I was saying.

I do remember that just before we got to the church the air suddenly smelled almost sweet, in a way it never had before, and I said, "What's that beautiful scent?"

"Lavender," she said. "It grows in the churchyard."

Maybe you've smelled lavender soap? This smelled drier and sunnier — that scent seemed all mixed up with the sun and Sunday and summer.

The church was gray stone, very old, and inside, cold, even that day. Banners that people had carried in real wars hung on the walls.

Church was the only time at Sibton Park that I was bored. Of course, we weren't allowed to talk; we weren't allowed even to read the other parts of the prayer book or the words of the other hymns. We had to just look at the page in the book that we were on. Sometimes hymns are loud and fun, but if we sang too loudly in church, Marza got cross (the Sunday before we'd really bellowed "Onward Christian Soldiers").

The only things to do in church were say the prayers, sing the hymns, and think.

After church, we went to our form rooms to write our letters to our parents. If you were a junior, your form mistress read your letter and corrected any mistakes; you wrote it over if there were any and then she read it again. When it was passed you could play until dinner time. No one read the seniors' letters.

That Sunday I wrote two letters, one to Emmy and one to the rest of the family. But first, I reread their letters to me: My mother had already written me twelve letters, and Emmy had written me one. Willy and Bubby each sent a letter, too, but not real letters — Bubby's was pretend writing (two pages of scribbles about the size of letters) and Willy's was a picture with his name in capital letters and X's for kisses.

This is Emmy's letter; she drew a picture on the back of it, too.

Philip was the pet budgerigar they had promised her — my mother had written to me about getting him, and that they had started a new school.

I had written to her first:

Dear Emmy,

I'm having a wonderful time. You are allowed to go into the fields and pet the horses. I wish you were here with me. It isn't very long until May 16th. There are four children in my dormitory counting me: their names are Clare, Veryan, and Brioney. If you came you would be in the 1st form. I am in 2B. I would be in 2A probably if it wasn't for my French. What are you doing? Are you smart in school? Can't wait until May 16th.

Love, Libby.

My mother's last letter was:

Dear Libby —

We all hope you are having a good time.

Great excitement here this week as Emmy and Willy started their new school, and guess who else did? Bubby! Bubby will go only in the mornings. Emmy and Willy will have every Wednesday afternoon as a half-holiday, and their half-term holiday will be the same as yours. They all enjoyed school; liked their teachers and the other children. It's a very nice school and I think all three will learn a lot and have a good time, too.

Have the clothes we ordered arrived yet? You should be receiving your riding clothes, ballet tunic, mac, and another skirt. When we come to visit you, we can bring along anything you may have forgotten to pack if you will let us know what you want. Will bring along your other jumper, too. Are your pajamas warm enough, Libby?

Bubby considers herself quite grown up now that she has started school. She was very shy about going into her classroom the first day, later told us she had played with plasticene, gone out in the garden, taken a rest, listened to a story, and played with a horse.

Be sure to let us know if there is anything you need or want, and we can bring it when we come to see you on the 16th. Love from all of us, dear.

Mother

I wrote this to everyone else:

Dear Mother and Father and Willy and Bubby,

How are you? Mo says Bubby's writing looks exactly like Persian. So Bubby may be writing in Persian and we don't know it! We have lessons on Saturday until 12:30. Are you pleased with how smart Emmy is? At night we play a game called Hospital. We made it up. We use my nail set for the doctor's tools. The operation we did last night was appendix. With a blunt thing we poked around, with the sharp one we gave shots, one that is like a scraper we use to open the skin. With the tweezers we take out the appendix, with the nail file we take the patient's temperature and with the scissors (the handles of them) we sew it up. The title of the hymn book I need is The Common Prayer Hymns Ancient and Modern. When will my riding clothes be ready? Give my love to everyone.

Love, Libby.

Then I put some kisses and hugs at the bottom. I would be seeing them on Saturday, May 16th, one day less than two weeks away — not VERY long.

Chapter Twenty-one: My First Riding Lesson

Finally my riding clothes came: thick brown jodhpurs, a tweed jacket, string gloves, and a hard hat. I didn't need boots — most juniors rode in their walking shoes.

Clare on Frisky. They are in the stable yard; Miss Monkman is in the stable doorway.

I was VERY excited. In my class were Brioney, someone who was only five, and Clare. They had all ridden before — quite a lot — and Clare had real jodhpur boots.

We started in the stable yard — I had Tuppence. Miss Monkman showed me how to get on (it was much easier with a stirrup and saddle), and she made the stirrups the right length and put my feet in them; she pushed my heels down and told me to keep them down. She pushed my lower legs back a bit and pressed my knees into the saddle, and then she put my fingers around the reins, so that my two fists were facing each other with the thumbs on top, and the bottoms of my fists were pressed into

Tuppence. She said, "Whatever you do, don't let go of the reins —
even if you fall off."

She glanced at the others, told Brioney to shorten her stirrups,
and then, with Tuppence's reins in one hand, she led us out of the
stable yard. We walked down the road, through the cow pasture, and
into the horse pasture, with Miss Monkman holding my reins and
talking to me the whole time. Finally when we got to the paddock, she
let go of the reins and let me ride by myself.

I was really riding. I was on a horse, I could feel it moving underneath me, and see its mane kind of flapping up and down, and its
ears flickering back and forth — listening, maybe wondering who
I was.

I tried to keep the reins where Miss Monkman had put them: in
my fists, with my thumbs on top, and the bottom of my hands on the
pony's withers (two bumpy bones right in front of the saddle). I held
my hands still, so I wouldn't hurt Tuppence's mouth — Miss
Monkman told me that, and I remembered what *Black Beauty* said
about the bit, too. I pushed my toes up and my heels down.

I gripped with my knees. I sat up straight and looked straight
ahead, between Tuppence's flickering ears, keeping my elbows
pressed to my sides.

I could do all those things at once while we walked.

Then Miss Monkman, who was standing in the middle of the
paddock while we rode round her, called, "Trot!" and all the horses

went faster and Tuppence did, too. I bumped up and down, wobbling all over the place and almost losing my balance — my arms went out, my hands jerked off the withers and into the air; but I didn't let go of the reins.

"Libby, grab the saddle or a bit of mane if you feel yourself losing your balance! Sit up straight!" Miss Monkman shouted. "Keep your hands on the withers!"

I tried to but I kept bumping up and down and so did my hands.

"Heels down, Libby — it's easier to balance that way!" Miss Monkman said. "Post."

(That means watch the outside shoulder — when it goes forward, push yourself up. You can pretend there's a string from the horse's shoulder to the middle of your belt, pulling you up and forward. Miss Monkman had explained all that but it's hard to do.)

"It's a RHYthm. ONE two, ONE two. Up! Down! Post — one, two! One, two! Up, down! Count with me, come on."

I watched and counted — ONE two, ONE two — but I still bumped. Once or twice I did actually post in rhythm — I think, I'm not sure. Most of the time I just jostled around, but I did stay on.

There was so much to think about and try to do all at once. Riding was MUCH harder than I expected; the only thing that was easy was sitting up straight.

The next day my bottom and the inside of my thighs hurt quite a lot. I asked Clare about it.

"You're saddle-sore," Clare said. "It's because riding is new to you."

"I'm not very good at it," I said.

"You will be once you can post," she said. I asked how long that would take. She said, "Posting is a bit like riding a bicycle — one day you just do it and after that you always know."

I tried to remember how long it had taken to learn to ride a two-wheeler, but I couldn't; and riding a horse seemed much harder. But I'd learn.

Chapter Twenty-two: May 16th

On Saturday, May 16th, right after lessons, I waited in the corridor by the Tudor Garden: this was where people always waited for their parents when they were being taken out. I knew that because lots of people already had gone out. It was only in your first term that you weren't allowed to see your parents for the first six weeks.

There was a door with glass panes at the top: You could see the Tudor Garden and beyond it, the front drive.

I waited and waited, listening for a car. I had written them where I would be waiting, and written them again on Wednesday to remind them of the date and time.

While I was waiting, Sarah Riley came by and asked me what kind of car they had.

"I don't know," I said. She looked surprised, and I added, "It's a different one every time they go someplace."

"Oh, you hire a car, do you?" she said — she sort of drawled the words and pronounced "hire" as though it was "har" in a way that made me uncomfortable.

Finally I heard a car in the distance slow down, and then saw it turn into the driveway. I got to the car before anyone got out.

"Mummy!" I shouted. "Mummy!"

Emmy made a little face at me (because of the "Mummy," I knew).

I asked if I could show Emmy the horses, and my parents looked at each other. I had written to them about Nella that first day, and my riding lessons, but not about riding Tuppence.

"Oh, please can I?" she said.

"We'll be very careful," I said.

"Me come too?" Bubby said with a big smile, and we all laughed.

"You older girls may go if you promise to just look at the horses from over the fence: Don't go into the field."

We promised.

As soon as we could talk privately, Emmy looked at me and said, "*Mummy?*"

"Well, that is how it's pronounced in England," I said. "We usually stand on the fence like this."

I put my feet on the bottom rail and held the top one; Emmy did, too. We leaned over the fence and watched the horses eating grass in the sun. I told Emmy all their names, and about my riding lessons (I'd had several by then).

"It's much harder than I thought it would be," I said. "But I'm getting better: I can ALMOST post."

I explained what posting was, and told her about riding Tuppence in the field that day, and she laughed, but when I asked her if she'd like to come to Sibton Park, too, she said no, she'd rather stay at home.

Bubby in the back seat with her birthday teddy.

"If you came you could take riding lessons — we have three each week. And you could pet the horses whenever you wanted to," I said. "I come into this field almost every day."

"It's good — but, I don't want to leave home," Emmy said.

When we got into the car, Bubby proudly showed me her new teddy bear (it was almost as big as she was).

"My birthday teddy," she said. "I'm three."

She DID seem older. She seemed like a person, not a baby.

A lot of other things had changed at home, too. Jill was gone, they had moved (which I knew from my mother's letters), but my father told me anyway, adding, "The new apartment has a big garden the children can play in."

"Do you play in it?" I said.

"Sometimes," Emmy said.

Bubby and Willy didn't answer: They were talking to each other (or her new teddy and his old Raggedy Ann doll) in growly, very low voices and giggling, as usual. THAT hadn't changed.

Willy and Bubby in the back seat.

We went to an inn for lunch and ate in the garden, until it started to rain heavily. That happened a lot on English outings.

The first part of lunch at the inn. You can only see a little of Emmy—she's sitting between Willy and my mother, across the table from me.

After lunch, we drove back. Emmy wanted to go see the horses again, and I wanted to show them to Bubby and Willy, too; but it was time for them to go home and for me to be back at school, my father said.

I hugged him, and my mother, and Bubby, and Willy, and Emmy; and then they drove away. Emmy waved her arm back and forth across the whole rear window — I could see the gray sleeve of her sweater going back and forth until the car went out of sight.

Chapter Twenty-three:
"That Was My Father's Legion"

"You're awfully quiet today," Matron said at lunch the next day.

I still sat next to her at meals; everyone else wanted to sit next to her, too, so they took turns sitting on her other side. To make it fair, everyone but me sat in the same order and at each meal, they all moved one place — like at the Mad Tea Party in *Alice in Wonderland*.

I liked Matron as much as everyone else did, maybe more! But I didn't like *having* to sit next to her because of my manners. I wanted to be able to eat the way everyone else ate.

"I'm concentrating on eating properly," I said. Soup you had to tilt into your mouth, with the spoon sideways. Only the very edge of the spoon could touch your lips.

Matron laughed.

"But that's no good! You must carry on a conversation *and* eat properly." It was like riding, I thought: everything all at the same time. "Tell us where the Koponens are going for the summer holidays."

That's what they had been talking about: where everyone was going for the holidays. Matron's parents and Clare were all going to Greece.

"To a farm in Cornwall for part of the time," I said. "They're not sure about the rest of the holidays. My father wants to take my mother to Italy, but they haven't found a new nanny yet, so there's no one to take care of us."

"I'll look after you!" Matron said eagerly.

I was VERY surprised — and pleased.

"I'll write and ask!" I said. "Oh, I hope they say yes!"

Clare and I talked about it while we stood on line for sweets and walked to the Lower Garden, where we had a story after lunch. Miss Davenport was already sitting in her chair under the old oak, waiting while everyone found places on the grass.

Sun coming through leaves made little wavering patches of light and shadows on the lawn. And it was so bright and sunny that when I sat down, even the grass felt warm! I looked up at the big branch high above us, then around the lawn, at the dappled light and all the girls in their striped summer dresses: white with pale blue stripes, white with pale pink, white with pale green — they all looked white in the pale bright sun. When everyone was still and quiet, Miss Davenport began to read.

It was a happy feeling, looking at the dappled light, listening to the story. It was about an English boy in ancient Britain, and I liked it until a grown-up in the book told about a Roman legion that marched off into the mist and never came back. They just disappeared. There was a pause and the boy said, "That was my father's legion."

I imagined him just standing there, watching his father's legion leave: men in tunics and metal helmets marching straight down a Roman road. That was the last time the boy ever saw his father—his father disappeared into the gray mist and never came back.

I saw that so clearly in my mind that I was almost surprised to look around me and see the old tree, the dappled light on the lawn, the faded pink house—surprised and glad. The old bricks' colors were soft and peaceful—beautiful, even—glowing in the sun. They'd been there for hundreds and hundreds of years. They were solid and safe.

> Dear Koponans
> Mother, I am glad you liked the egg cosy. The cross stitching was the first I've ever done.
> What do you think of Matron looking after us while you are in Italy. Emmy, Willa & Bobby would simply love her. She lives in a lovely big house in Lyminge. She said we could go and stay in her house. She has a dog & cat & some hens every morning she goes out and gathers their eggs I hope you will write to her soon and let her look after us. Just a few days ago she said she was twenty six and a half.
> Don't forget that July 11th is sports day. We had heats on Friday. The people who came in First, Second, Third or Fourth get to run

The letter I wrote asking about staying with Matron.

Chapter Twenty-four:
After Lights Out

The days got longer and longer: in England, the sky stays light almost all night in summer. When we went to bed it was still bright blue. The seniors had Lights Out much later — they were still outside when the sky had turned a strange silvery-white color and we were sitting up in bed, talking. If there was a pause in our conversation, we could hear them.

One night we talked, first about our running heats (we were practicing for Sports Day), and then about the Tennis Match. Juniors didn't play tennis, but we'd all watched it, the whole school had. The look on the loser's face was awful — and the loser was Jill, Buffer's twin sister.

"Buffer didn't even say anything to her," Veryan said.

"She didn't the day the seniors got their exams back, either," Clare said, sounding even more critical.

I remembered Buffer running up the back stairs two at a time, so fast that she was putting her hands on the steps ahead of her, laughing and screaming: "I pahssed! I pahssed!"

Jill had not passed. She spent the whole afternoon crying in Alice and Tina's room, being comforted by them — and Buffer ignored her.

"I hated Buffer that day," Veryan said.

"So did I," Brioney said.

"She was selfish," said Clare.

I didn't hate Buffer, but I did remember how the other seniors had acted. Alice and Tina passed, everyone knew they would; I don't think anyone even asked them. Someone asked two other seniors if they'd passed. One looked a little embarrassed — as if she hadn't really deserved to—and said yes. The other smiled, trying to be casual, but you could tell she was pleased. Only Buffer ran around screaming and laughing and telling people who hadn't even asked her. I understood that you shouldn't behave like that, ever; but I didn't know if Jill being her own twin made it worse. I was wondering about that when we heard Matron laughing outside (of course, the windows were all open).

We all went to the same window and looked out. Miss Davenport and Matron were riding in the big meadow that sloped up to a skyline of trees. The sky was that strange light silvery color — not like day, but not like night, either — and their horses, Nella and Nike, looked silvery-white, too.

Suddenly Matron leaned forward in the saddle and shook her head, and first Nella, then Nike, GALLOPED towards the top of the meadow, stretching out their necks and tails while Matron shrieked with laughter.

Matron's laugh got fainter and fainter as they raced farther and farther away, the horses' tails streaming behind them.

We stood close together, watching. No one talked until we couldn't see them anymore and were slowly getting back into bed.

"I didn't know Matron rode," Clare said quietly.

I hadn't, either. I listened for Matron and the horses while the room grew dimmer; on the towel rack, I could see the white part of my towel, but not the colors of its gray and red stripes. I listened hard, but the only sounds were some seniors playing tennis: a ball being hit, someone calling "BAD luck!" and a piano — probably other seniors were rehearsing the play. None of us were in that (only one junior, a four-year-old day girl, was), and suddenly I had the idea of putting on our own play. ONLY the Night Nursery would be in it and we'd make it up ourselves.

In the morning I told the others, and everyone wanted to do it. In bed that night, we decided to make the play about doctors and nurses falling in love with each other (this, I admit, was kind of copied from an English TV show). The first thing we made up was a song about them falling in love, which Brioney and Clare and Veryan sang in American accents, one verse each. I just hummed the chorus.

Veryan made up a song to sing by herself. Her idea was that she would march down the aisle, dressed in a bride's outfit, filing her nails with the file from my manicure kit, singing:

> I'll be walking' down the aisle
> with a smile
> filin' me nails with me file.

She got out of bed to show us. I had to laugh: She filed her nails so briskly and looked so businesslike about the whole thing, and the words were so ridiculous! Once we started working on "Emergency Ward Eleven: A Love Story," after Lights Out was hilarious: we laughed and laughed. We rehearsed every night, and the whole school came to the performance — even all the seniors came. At the end they clapped and clapped, and some people shouted "Bravo!" and "Encore!" and "Author, Author!" Even though it was only in the Nursery, and not on a real stage, everyone acted just as if we were all grown-up and at the theater.

Chapter Twenty-five: "Going Home Tomorrow!"

It was the last day of summer term: All the people who were going home by car (most of the school) had already left, so the rest of us were all put in the same wing. I was in Trafalgar, a big dormitory down the hall from Nelson, where I'd spent that first night. Hazel Fogarty was there, too, with other fourth- and fifth-formers — Clare and Brioney and Veryan had gone home by car.

It was also the night before my birthday. At Sibton Park on the night before your birthday, two people from your dormitory went around to all the other dormitories with a pillow case, and everyone who liked you put in a little present. Then when you woke up on the morning of your birthday, the two girls from your dormitory who had gone around gave you the pillowcase, which was always called "your sack." But I wasn't in my own dormitory, and everyone from it had already gone home, so I wouldn't be having one.

Because the Trafalgar girls were in the fourth or fifth form, Lights Out was much later. Everyone seemed very excited. They jumped up and down on their beds singing — practically shouting — a song with a lively tune:

One more day of pain,
One more day of sorrow,
One more day of this old dump,
We're going home tomorrow!

I was a little surprised to see Linda Jay shouting and laughing —
I don't think I'd ever even seen her smile before. She had long blonde
braids and hair cut straight across her forehead. She was the best rider
in the school; that made sense to me because her hair — those
braids, that fringe — made you think of horses. Also she had very
long legs and her mouth was long and determined-looking, too.
Linda Jay and Foggy were best friends. They sang the song again.

Foggy said, "Come on, Libby! Sing!"

So I did. We sang and jumped up and down and threw pillows at
each other until Matron came in and turned out the light; after that
they just talked. I don't remember the conversation: I must have
fallen asleep at the very beginning of it, which was unusual. In the
Night Nursery I was always the last one to fall asleep — by far.

When I woke up the next morning it was hot and sunny, and
Linda Jay and Hazel Fogarty were standing next to my bed, both
smiling, with their hands behind their backs.

"Happy birthday, Libby!"

"Many happy returns!" everyone said, and Linda Jay handed me
a white pillowcase — a sack!

I was too surprised and happy to say anything.
"Your sack," Linda said.

I looked inside and then took the things out
one by one. There was a book from Catherine
Marshall; a little notebook from Matron with a
note about writing (and seeing me soon); little
things people had made; a pencil; a pen; jacks; a
little vase for dolls' flowers . . . there were so many
presents — EVERYONE must have put some-
thing in. I was surprised and very, very pleased that so many people
liked me.

The little doll's vase
from the sack.

Then we all sang:

> *One more day of pain,*
> *One more day of sorrow,*
> *One more day of this old dump,*
> *We're going HOME toMORrow!*

Foggy FLUNG her sheet into the air — it billowed out sunny and
white and then floated down slowly, full of light —
"TODAY!"

Chapter Twenty-six:
At the Vicarage

Emmy, Bubby, and me in Cornwall.

My parents' new apartment didn't seem at all like home, but we didn't stay there long: We went to Cornwall and then to Matron's. She said to call her Veronica, and she had a brother about Emmy's age! His name was Barnabus; Veronica called him Barny. He was blond and plump and seemed to like having us there.

They lived in an old house — not as big as Sibton Park, but big, with lots of halls and passageways and a room just for books. There was a big overgrown garden with a swing, and at the back, a fenced-in yard for a flock of chickens!

Emmy and Bubby, of course, thought this was great and spent most of their time playing there. They ran around the house clucking and giggling, too. They had become very good friends — they slept in the same room and Veronica let them sleep in the same bed. She also let them feed the chickens and find their eggs.

I didn't like the chickens: They were very smelly and, I thought, quite stupid. Barny didn't like them either. He said, "Before you came, I had to go into the hen house and get the eggs every morning. I hated it!"

He usually played with Willy. Sometimes I played with them, but usually I talked to Veronica or read on the first-floor landing. It had dark green–patterned wallpaper — very old, Veronica had told me. It went well with the house, I thought: branches from all the old trees around it came right up to the windows. One morning I was lying there, reading — with that green wallpaper and those leafy branches it was almost like reading in a tree house. Downstairs, I could hear Veronica typing (she was writing a novel and we talked about it every afternoon). I heard Willy and Barny playing in the small draw-ing room; after a while, I decided to go down and see what they were doing.

They were playing an old-fashioned, by-hand version of pinball, which they called backgammon. They played this over and over, al-most every day! They were playing when I went in: Willy was shoot-ing and Barny was holding a pad of paper. They both looked very serious.

"Shh!" Barnabus said. "He needs to concentrate on his shot!"

Willy looked almost scared as he flicked the marble. Then: "BAD luck!" Barnabus said, in that polite, cheerful English way. "My turn!"

I looked at the pad: There were lots of points for Barnabus, none for Willy.

I went outside: Emmy and Bubby were, of course, in the chicken yard — I could hear them laughing and clucking.

I could have gone in — or asked them to come out — but I didn't. I didn't really mind playing alone. After all, if I wanted to talk to someone I could always talk to Veronica, or write to Henry.

Instead, I got on the long, old-fashioned swing — it went up really high.

I was swinging my hardest, singing loudly. (The night before, Veronica had taken me — only me — to a village sing; I was singing an English song I'd learned there called "Green Grow the Rushes, O!" When no one can hear me, I like to sing.) I was seeing if I could get high enough to touch a branch on the next tree with my toe when I heard Veronica calling me.

I dragged my feet on the ground to stop the swing — in America when we did that we always used to say, "Let the old cat die!" (I don't know why) — and ran in.

"Green Grow the Rushes, O!" is *fun to sing — almost like a game. The leader sings:*
"I'll sing you a one-o, green grow the rushes, o!"

Then everyone else sings:
"What is your one-o?"

The leader sings back:
"One is one and all alone and ever more shall be so.
I'll sing you a two-o, green grow the rushes, o!"
"What is your two-o?"
"Two, two the lily white boys, clothed all in green-o,
One is one and all alone and ever more shall be so!"
(It goes up to twelve.)

"My parents are coming back early," she said. "They'll be here late tonight."

"I thought they were going to be gone for the whole time," I said.

"They were."

It IS kind of fun to be at home without any grown-ups. It was odd; at Sibton Park Veronica had seemed grown up, but here she seemed more like our American teenage baby-sitters, only I liked her even more than I liked them.

> To make a hospital corner, you pull the sheet out, then tuck in the bottom part. Then you pull the top, folding it in a sort of triangle, and tuck it in very tightly and tidily.

"Well!" Veronica said very briskly. "Let's see what sort of state your rooms are in."

"I'll help you tidy up!" I said, and I did.

The most interesting part was putting clean sheets on her parents' bed. She showed me how to make real hospital corners, and the sheets smelled exactly like the sunny lavender on the walk to church. When I said so, Veronica said, "It *is* that lavender. Mummy dries it and puts it in the linen cupboard."

That was the only thing she said about her parents.

When I came into the dining room the next morning, Veronica's mother, a faded gray woman — her face was pale and her hair was pale and kind of messy — was sitting at one end of the table. Barny, Willy, Bubby, Emmy, and Veronica were at the other.

I thought the politest thing to do would be to sit next to

Veronica's mother, so I did. I smiled politely, too, and waited for her to say something.

She looked around, in a bewildered sort of way.

"MUST we have the bottle on the table?" she said. (This was a large milk bottle at the children's end of the table.) "It looks so . . ."

She stopped talking and waved her hand kind of helplessly, as though she couldn't think of a word. At home we never had the bottle on the table, either — my mother always put the milk into a pitcher. I started to say that, but then I thought that would make it seem WORSE that we had done it here; so I looked at the floor (big black and white tiles — I liked them) and then out the windows. The dining room had long windows opening onto the lawn.

I wondered if Veronica's mother liked us being there. Veronica didn't say anything: She just picked up the milk bottle, carried it into the kitchen, and came back with a pitcher. She didn't say a word.

I was making my bed, with hospital corners, when I heard a scream from the next room, Emmy and Bubby's room.

I ran in. Veronica's mother was standing in front of an open drawer, and in the drawer, squawking and flapping its wings, was — a chicken!

It looked so ridiculous, and Veronica's mother looked so astonished, that I laughed. But then, when I saw the mother's face closer up, I stopped quickly.

"Don't be afraid," I said in what I hoped was a calming English voice. "It's only a chicken. My sisters must have put it there — they're mad about all animals, even chickens. They're young and not very sensible yet."

Veronica's mother nodded and then sat down on the bed, suddenly.

I looked in the drawer: There was some chicken feed sprinkled on the bottom and a bowl with a little water left in it. The rest of the water had spilled: You could see a big wet spot on the paper. It WAS the kind of thing, exactly the kind of thing, that Emmy and Bubby would have done.

Veronica came running in, and her mother said, sounding VERY angry, "Veronica, those children have put a HEN in a drawer! This is really —"

Veronica grabbed the hen and shoved it at me. "Libby, take this back to the chicken yard."

I took it in both hands, holding my arms out straight in front of me to keep it as far away from me as I could. The feathers felt slightly greasy, and under THEM it was warm and wriggling; and (worst of all) solid and squishy at the same time. It also smelled horrible.

I turned my face away from it, but no matter what I did, I could feel it wriggling hotly under my hands. It was heavy, too.

I wasn't listening, but I couldn't help hearing Veronica say, "But, Mummy!"

Then her mother (who had a very quiet voice, even when she was angry) said something and Veronica said, "I think they've done him a lot of good!"

Her mother must have said something about our influence on Barny.

I got to the chicken yard and sort of threw the chicken over the gate. It flapped its wings as it landed, but didn't really fly.

Emmy and Bubby came running up.

"Did you put that hen in the drawer?"

Emmy nodded.

"What on Earth did you do that for?" I said.

Emmy and Bubby giggled, and I realized I DID sound sort of too English — like a schoolmistress! I hadn't been trying to sound English; when I first went to Sibton Park, I did try with my accent — very hard; but now, I didn't have to try. I just sounded English.

But I really was curious.

"Why?" I said. "Why did you do it?"

"I thought it would be nice for Philip to have another bird's company," Emmy said. "Someone to talk to."

Of all the idiotic reasons!

"Couldn't you just have brought HIS cage out here?"

"I didn't think of that."

Then Bubby said something in their chicken language, and they went on with their game, whatever it was.

I went back inside and found Veronica.

"Was your mother VERY cross about the hen?"

"More startled," Veronica said. "She's not used to American children. How would you like to go to the seaside today?"

American children! As though we were worse than other kinds! And her mother DIDN'T like having us there.

I decided that when I grew up, I'd never make guests feel unwelcome, even if they were — especially if the guests were children from another country.

But *Veronica* liked us, especially me. She had stuck up for us, too.

"That sounds fun," I said, trying to sound like it would be.

I knew what the English beach was like: cold, with gray, not blue, water and tiny waves. Instead of sand there were little pebbles — but still, it was the ocean!

When we got there, Veronica told us that waves with white curling tops are called "prancing ponies." Emmy and Bubby loved that.

They ran up to the little waves holding hands and then, shrieking and giggling, ran away from them. I was about to dive in (I love to swim) when Veronica said, "Oh, look! A wishing pebble!"

She picked up a pure white — almost transparent — pebble.

"When I was a child, we believed that you could make wishes on white stones."

"One wish for each stone?"

She nodded.

"You throw the stone into the sea and make a wish."

I decided to find a white stone and wish to go back to America. In Cornwall, my father had talked a lot about how much he loved

London and what a "great life" it was for them and for another American couple they knew. My mother didn't say anything until he used this couple as an example. Then she said: "Yes, it's a great life for Helen — lugging the coal scuttle up from the basement!"

It sounded as though she didn't want to stay, either, but I was still worried. I liked Veronica, and lots of things in England were interesting and fun, but I didn't belong here.

So, I looked for white pebbles. The sun came out for a minute, and the pebbles all shone — there seemed to be quite a lot of almost white ones. The others were holding hands and trying to jump over the waves, but I kept looking for white pebbles.

I found one and ran to the water. I faced west, where America was, thinking of a long, straight line, with me at one end and America at the other. Then I threw the stone into the gray water, straight towards America, towards Henry and home, and wished.

Chapter Twenty-seven: Back at Sibton

But when I got back to Sibton Park for Autumn Term, we were all a little bit excited to see each other again, and I was extra-excited because I'd done so well in all my subjects, including French, that I was going to be in IIA, not IIB! Then, when we were in the cloakroom changing into our house shoes (it was one of those warm fall days and we'd been playing outside), something even more exciting happened.

I was on the floor tugging off my Wellingtons when someone came running in shouting, "We've got a study! IIA has its own study!"

We'd never had a study before, only the older girls had them. I'd never even been in one — they're private, that's the whole point. In school stories they have fireplaces and the girls roast chestnuts and make tea and have little parties in them.

Wellingtons

"Hooray!" I said.

That sounds fake, but it's the kind of thing people say in England when they're happy. It didn't SOUND as happy as I felt, though, so I kicked my Wellington the rest of the way off — off, and up in the air — hard.

It flew up and then out through the (closed) window, smashing the pane completely.

Everyone kind of gasped.

I stood up.

"Where are you going?" Clare said.

"To own up, of course," I said.

She gave that little Clare half smile — as though something was amusing.

I didn't find Marza, but I did find her mother, an old lady we didn't see much who always wore black dresses down to her ankles. I told her my name and then what I had done. She said, "I'm sure Marza will understand."

She didn't.

About half an hour later, she sent for me. When I went into her office she was sitting up very straight, as usual. (She told us once that her posture was so good because when she was a girl they had to wear special things on their backs to MAKE them straight. Hers had worked, I guess: I never saw her back touch a chair.)

She just looked at me without saying anything for what felt like a long time. I could see that she was quite cross. When she asked me how I had broken the window, her voice sounded a little like all the mothers in America when these things happened and they said things like, "What were you doing with the record on your head, Libby?"

But when I'd finished talking and Marza said, "That wasn't very sensible, was it?" I minded. I admired Marza.

Then she asked me, sounding kind of curious, why I had done it.

"I was just so excited about our getting a study," I said, and that sounded feeble (that's what they say in England — it's a good word, I think) even to me.

She said that when "one" did things that were "foolish or un-guarded" or "thoughtless," someone else usually had to "bear the consequences." In this case, she said, someone else would have to mend the window. She also talked about being "sensible" and "careful."

"You have high spirits," she said (and the way she said that made it sound as though high spirits weren't a bad thing to have), "but you must learn to be sensible and have self-command or your heedless-ness will be a source of grief to you as well as to others."

That was probably true, I thought.

"I will," I said. "Well, I'll try."

"Very well then, off you go."

When she said that, she didn't sound so cross. I *would* try, I thought.

Chapter Twenty-eight:
Trying

I started trying right away.

On the first day of lessons, Miss Tomlinson, the teacher, put me in the first row, the row closest to her desk. IIA's class and classroom were bigger than IIB's, and everyone was my age or older. Some of the girls in the back looked a lot older; at least, they were a lot bigger.

Lessons started the same way, with Scripture; but instead of telling us what chapter to do, Miss Tomlinson said, "From now on, instead of just describing what happens in the chapter, you're to explain what it means." Some people looked a little confused. "Just write what the chapter says, as usual, and then explain the meaning. You'll need to think a bit."

She smiled when she said the last part, and then told us to go to Luke, Chapter 19. I read the chapter quickly — I always like reading and writing, and I liked the idea of saying what we thought it meant. I read the chapter and I thought I really DID know what it meant.

Eagerly, as fast as I could, but in my best handwriting, I wrote:

> The Parable of the ten Pieces of silver
> Jesus was having supper, and he
> told a parable and this is what it
> was: "There was a man who was rich,
> and he went away to another kingdom
> and he called his ten servants before
> him; and he gave each of them a pound
> and told them to trade it and make it
> more. Then he went and when he came back
> he asked the first servant what he had
> made and He said, 'I have made ten
> pounds.' and then the first one was rewarded
> with ten cities. The second one had five pounds
> and was rewarded with five cities. The third
> had ropped'd up in a napkin and he gained
> nothing. The master said he was wicked. He gave
> him no reward and he had to give his pound to
> the one who got ten pounds. Then he had to pay
> the money that that master would have got if he had
> put it in the bank. The story means that we all have
> talents and if we don't use them they'll be taken away
> from us.

wrapped

Miss Tomlinson corrected our Scripture while we did our arithmetic.

Then, looking annoyed, she said only one person had done her
Scripture properly. "And on her very first day, too."

I was the only new person, so it must have been me. Everyone
looked at me, some people not in a very friendly way — a girl in
my new dormitory, Jennifer Dixon, looked especially cold. (My new
dormitory was called Florence Nightingale. Brioney was still in the
Night Nursery, with other younger children, but I was in Florence

Nightingale and everyone in the dormitory was in IIA: Clare, Veryan, Jennifer Dixon, and me. I was in a dormitory AND a class, IIA, with the other people my own age.)

I felt relieved that I would be able to do the lessons, and a bit odd: a teacher had never said anything good about me before. A bit odd is the English way of saying it, but that's how I thought by then; now, I would say it felt strange and a little uncomfortable, but nice, too. That made me want to try even more.

> FLORENCE NIGHTINGALE was a famous English lady and nurse. She was called "the lady of the lamp" because she carried a lamp around a hospital in one of the English wars — but she had also STARTED the whole hospital. Before that, they didn't have hospitals for the wounded soldiers.
>
> Once, a man in the government had said, "It can't be done," and Florence Nightingale just looked at him calmly and said, "But it must be done."
>
> The man said he never forgot the force of those words. And whatever it was got done.

The rest of the lessons were just as interesting as in IIB, and harder. We read Shakespeare. I said I didn't see what was so great about him; Miss Tomlinson said I would understand when I was grown up.

The coats, but not the hats, we wore: This is from a recent school catalog.

She seemed to find my comments more interesting than Miss Davenport had (maybe Scripture got things off to a lucky start?).

Now when we went to church we wore brown-and-white checked coats and brown velvet hats and brown wool gloves, and sat as close together as we could. I still thought church was boring, but I tried to understand what it was all about.

I knew the words of all the prayers and hymns. Usually the hymns were quiet. Often they had something in them about Jesus being crucified — nails in his ankles and arms and a crown of thorns on his head. All that blood and suffering, and prayers about miserable sinners — I didn't like that at all.

There were some happy hymns, and I liked them:

> *All things bright and beautiful*
> *All creatures great and small*
> *All things wise and wonderful*
> *The Lord God made them all.*
> *Each little flower that opens*
> *Each little bird that sings*
> *He made their glowing colors*
> *He made their shining wings.*

This hymn had one verse that I didn't like:

> *The rich man in his castle*
> *The poor man at the gates*
> *God put them in their places*
> *And ordered their estates.*

That was the bad side of England — what the Revolution stopped in America — but they still had it in England. It reminded me of someone's father saying indignantly, ". . . when a shopkeeper starts thinking he's your equal!"

There were some quiet hymns I liked. One began:

> *For the beauty of the earth*
> *For the blessings of the field . . .*

The earth IS beautiful — around Sibton Park it was, anyway; why couldn't all the hymns be about that? Another one was about England's "green and pleasant" land and "clouded hills." That IS what England looks like ("clouded hills" always made me think of the horses' meadow, sloping up to trees at the top), so I liked it, too.

But although I WANTED to believe in God, and tried to believe, I just didn't see how there could be someone up in the sky who cared about everyone. But maybe it was true, in ways I couldn't understand. I couldn't understand how space could go on forever — but it did.

I wondered a lot if all the English children believed; I thought probably they did — God seemed so English. It seemed as though they thought God had blessed England in a special way and that in church they were worshipping England as much as God.

There were hymns and prayers about English sailors:

> *O hear us when we cry to thee*
> *For those in peril on the sea . . .*

and soldiers:

> *Our fathers heard the trumpet call*
> *From lowly cot and castle wall . . .*

and the English ruling foreign lands:

> *From Greenland's icy mountain*
> *To India's coral strand . . .*

The hymns gave a picture of English people all over the world, ruling it and being protected by God. In America we only had God on money and in the Pledge of Allegiance, but in England, even the national anthem was called "God Save the Queen." I *know* Marza believed, in England and in God. You could tell by the way she said the prayers every morning, even by the way she walked into prayers. Maybe, I thought, if I were English I'd believe, too — but I wasn't and I didn't.

Chapter Twenty-nine:
Little Women

Clare and I were both ill and had to stay in bed all day — it was fun. We talked all morning without stopping, and I was wondering how to ask her what *she* thought about God when Matron (the *new* Matron — just a typical grown-up, not bad, not good) brought our dinners in on trays.

As soon as she left Clare said, "Do you bother with proper manners when you're alone?"

I wasn't sure what to say; finally I decided it would be safe to tell the truth.

"No," I said.

She looked relieved and happy.

"Shall we eat with our fingers, then?" she said.

We did — REALLY messily. We didn't even wipe our faces or fingers at all until we were all done. It was a lot of fun and I was really glad I'd said no. And we talked about books: One of the most fun things about Sibton Park was that everyone read a lot so you could talk about books with people and they would say things back. In America I could never do that. We talked about *Little Women* (it was one of her favorites, too).

I told her about a book I'd taken out from the library in America. A girl in this book was getting married to an old man. Her little sister didn't want her to. She said so and someone else in the book said, "Oh, I think it's so romantic — think of Jo and Professor Baer." The little sister said, "I always wanted her to marry Laurie."

In real life, another child who had taken that book out of the library had written in the margin: "Me too." So I got a pencil and wrote under HER writing, "So did I." (I always thought that was neat: a little club of girls who didn't know each other all thinking the same thing and telling each other, in a book.)

Jo not marrying Laurie, from an old copy of Little Women.

Clare said, "I wanted Jo to marry Laurie, too: Everyone does."

Then I told her that I had always thought I was like Jo. She gave me one of those sensible, considering English looks.

"I think you're more like Amy," she said.

Amy! She wasn't a writer, she wasn't a tomboy; and she was so selfish and so ridiculous, using all those big words and sleeping with a clothespin on her nose. How could anyone think I was like that?

Maybe it was because I tried so hard at everything — to talk and eat properly, to ride well, to be really good at lessons, especially French — and Amy tried hard, too. Jo didn't care what other people thought: the book said Jo "walked through life with her elbows sticking out," but Amy wanted people to like and admire her, and at Sibton Park, I did, too. But I didn't think anyone knew that — I didn't even really know it myself until Clare said I was like Amy, if that's what she meant. I didn't ask her: I was too hurt to say anything.

Chapter Thirty: Guy Fawkes

It was Guy Fawkes Day and everyone was at the bonfire. I wasn't going because I had wrecked my mackintosh. I'm not sure if this was a punishment (to teach me to be more careful and sensible) or just that everyone else was wearing theirs and I didn't have one. Anyway I wasn't going.

I was really CURIOUS about the bonfire and the guy (they burn a guy on the bonfire — I thought it was a kind of scarecrow but I wasn't

In England they have Guy Fawkes Day instead of Halloween. Guy Fawkes tried to blow up Parliament. He put lots of gunpowder underneath it — but it was discovered before it went off. They don't have trick-or-treating on Guy Fawkes Day: they have fireworks and bonfires.

sure, and that was one of the things I was curious about) and the fireworks — kinds we don't have in America. Roman Candles and Catherine Wheels sounded especially interesting — I pictured Roman Candles as like the Roman time candles we learned about in second grade (they were

A mackintosh is a warm, completely waterproof raincoat, with buttons and a belt. Our Sibton Park ones were tan on the outside and a brownish plaid on the inside, with rubber in between. Mackintoshes weren't always tan: Emmy, Willy, and Bubby's school had navy-blue ones.

striped and timed to burn for exactly an hour). But the fireworks, I thought, would also do something exciting: sparkle, maybe, or explode. Catherine Wheels I imagined as circles of fire revolving in the air, but I couldn't really imagine how they would work. So I was disappointed that I wouldn't see them — I was so curious, and I probably wouldn't be in England by the next Guy Fawkes Day.

But they were there, I wasn't; there was no sense in thinking about it.

I looked around the room, at the blue-and-white tiles by the fireplace (each tile was different), and at the pale yellow walls. The house was so quiet that I could hear the wind in the bare branches and even against the creepers that grew all over the outside walls.

It felt strange to be all by myself: not unpleasant, just strange — I'd never been all alone in the house before. I hadn't been by myself in a long time except to go to the loo, and that only takes a minute.

What about baths? you might think. We were together for those, too — each dormitory had its own time. There were four bathtubs in the room; each one had a curtain, but it was modest in a bad way to draw it so no one ever did. We played and talked while we had our baths.

Once, when I first came, Veryan turned on both faucets (they call them "taps") and then squatted and, pointing between her legs, said, "Three taps!"

Everyone laughed; I was a little bit shocked. At first I hadn't liked to take off my clothes in front of strangers, or have them see me in the bathtub, but by now I was used to these English ways.

I thought about how cozy our study was, and then I got out the story I was working on — I was hoping to finish it in time for Hobby Day. This was a day when things we had made were displayed in the Art Room. The whole school walked around and looked at them. My first term, mine looked very childish compared to the things the other girls had made.

But for THIS Hobby Day I was writing a story I hoped would be really good. It was called "The Richardsons" and it was already seventeen pages long — seventeen *big* pages, not composition-book pages (our composition books were only about half the size of regular big paper).

I hoped I could finish another chapter before the others came back and then read it to them. It felt snug to be writing in bed. After I'd been writing for a while I heard a lot of noise in the cloakroom downstairs, and soon everyone was running in. Their cheeks were all pink and they smelled of leaves and smoke and fresh air and everyone was talking at once. They described food they'd had, and then Clare pulled out her handkerchief tied up in a knot.

"We brought you some roast chestnuts," she said.

"And I smuggled out two roast potatoes!" said Jennifer.

That was so nice of them! And, while I was trying to get to sleep (I was the last one to fall asleep and the first one to wake up in this dormitory, too), thinking of smuggling those potatoes gave me an idea.

Chapter Thirty-one:
Food for a Feast

The next morning I told the idea to the others.

"Let's have a midnight feast!"

"With what food?" Jennifer said.

We talked it over: It wouldn't be as much fun with food from our meals, and we weren't allowed to go into the village. Then Clare said, "My parents are coming to take Carol and me out one Saturday. Perhaps I could go shopping."

We made a list of all the things we'd LIKE to get: lemon squash, Cadbury's chocolate fingers, butter, and lemon curd. Jennifer said that if Clare could get butter and lemon curd, the rest of us could stuff bread into our pockets at tea.

Clare told me privately that her parents had said that she and Carol could each bring a friend, and she had already decided to invite me. She had just been waiting for her parents to tell her when they were coming.

Finally the day came and Clare and I were sitting at a table in a restaurant with her parents, Colonel

Lemon curd comes in a jar and it looks like bright yellow jam. You put it on bread. It tastes kind of like sour lemon candies, or a lemon meringue pie filling that's not very sweet. Like many English foods, it sounds strange but tastes very good.

and Mrs. Sweeting, and Carol and her friend Georgina Miskin.

It was the first time I'd ever been to a grown-up restaurant without my parents. I think I did everything politely and ate everything properly.

Mrs. Sweeting did most of the talking. After a while she paused in her conversation and looked at Georgina's plate. Georgina had eaten everything except her Yorkshire pudding.

"Don't you like the Yorkshire pudding?" Mrs. Sweeting said.

"Actually it's my favorite thing," Georgina said politely. "I —"

"You like to save the best until last," Mrs. Sweeting said. Then, with a big smile, "How wise you are!"

I started to say that I did, too; and then I thought it would be better not to, so I didn't. That's one of the only times that I've started to say something and then stopped myself: I did it because I realized (very quickly, it was as though suddenly I saw myself from the outside) how — unbecoming, I guess you could call it, that remark would be: it would make me seem so pushy and greedy for attention!

The thought was much faster than that explanation, though. Afterwards I felt quite pleased that I had had the thought quickly enough to keep quiet.

Meanwhile, Clare's mother was talking about saving the best until last in life as well.

When we had put our knives and forks together, Clare said that we had an errand to do for the girls in our dormitory and could we go to the shop by ourselves, while everyone else had dessert?

Clare's mother and father both looked mildly surprised; Carol and Georgina looked at each other. Georgina (who I decided I didn't like very much) was smiling in kind of a superior way.

"It's rather a private errand," Clare said firmly, giving her sister and Georgina a cold look.

Her parents looked at each other, and then Mrs. Sweeting said we could go.

"Thank you very much for the lunch — dinner," I said. "It was delicious."

"I'm so glad you were able to come," Mrs. Sweeting said (in England they don't say "You're welcome").

Clare and I didn't talk to each other until we were outside.

"Do you feel proud to be out in your uniform?" she said. I thought about it.

"Yes," I said, finally. "Do you?"

She nodded.

We were in a little village, with a green in the middle of the street and old-fashioned shops with big windows divided up into lots of little panes. One had sweets in the window — we went in and found all the things.

While Clare was paying, I saw a little white box with pale shapes in different colors — hearts and bells and horseshoes — and CON-FETTI in pale blue capital letters.

"What is this?" I said eagerly. "What do you use it for?"

The woman smiled at me. She looked very nice, I thought.

"It's for weddings — when the bride and groom leave."

"People throw it," Clare said.

"That sounds fun!" I said.

The woman smiled again, opened the box, and gave it a little shake: Pale shapes floated slowly onto the counter — hearts and horseshoes and bells and what I now saw were meant to be wreaths, in all different cheerful colors.

"How beautiful," I said and then, thinking how perfect it would be for the midnight feast, "Let's get this, too!"

"But, it's for weddings."

"We can still throw it up in the air at our party!"

Chapter Thirty-two: The Midnight Feast

The alarm had probably been ringing for a long time when I woke up — I know in my dream a bell was ringing for quite a while.

When I woke all the way up the bell was still ringing. It took me a little while to figure out where I was, what the ringing sound was, and why I had set the alarm. By the time I had done that, the ringing had stopped and the hands of the clock pointed to six after midnight.

I sat up. The room was freezing (as usual, a window was open).

"Clare!" I whispered.

No answer.

"Jennifer!"

No answer.

"Veryan!"

No answer.

I got out of bed — it was REALLY cold — and put on my dressing gown (now I saw why the girls in the school stories always did!) and even my slippers.

English people were always talking, in books and real life, about how good for you "country air" was. That was probably why whoever put us to bed at Sibton Park always opened a window once we were under the blankets. Marza was very proud of how healthy we all were. My first term, Matron said once, "You were a pale London child, too, when you first came and now look at you! Marza was just saying yesterday how nice and rosy your cheeks have become!"

Then I went over to Clare's bed. I said her name a few times; she rolled over and went on sleeping. I shook her arm a little bit, then a bit harder. She opened her eyes, blinked a few times, then closed them again.

I grabbed her arm.

"Clare! The midnight feast!"

She nodded and sat up.

It took the two of us a long, long time to wake Veryan and Jennifer.

Finally we spread the feast on a blanket and sat down on it ourselves, huddled together in a little circle. A little light came in through the windows — from stars? a moon we couldn't see? No one had a torch: They were always confiscated, so old girls never even bothered to bring them.

> Things we weren't supposed to have — like torches — were taken away and locked up by Matron. This was called being "confiscated." You got the things back at the end of term.

At first, we didn't talk much: Everyone kept yawning and yawning, you could hear them. Then, I said, "Let's have a toast! It's true that we don't have any glasses, but we can all hold a swallow of lemon squash in our mouths. The last person can say the toast and then we can clink hands — like this." I made a loose fist and raised it, the way grown-ups raise their wineglasses, and lightly touched it to my other hand. "When we've all done it to each other, we'll swallow the lemon squash! It will be a real toast, just without wineglasses."

"All right," Clare said. "Who's going to make the toast?"

"I will," Jennifer said.

It was hard not to giggle after we had taken our sips and passed the bottle to the next person, but no one did. Jennifer raised the bottle, and we raised our fists while she said the toast. Then she took a sip and we clinked fists (exactly the way grown-ups clink wineglasses), swallowed, and all started laughing.

"Let's sing something," Veryan said.

Everyone thought this was a good idea; we started with a song from singing class we all liked:

> *Early one morning*
> *Just as the sun was rising*
> *I heard a maiden sing in the valley below.*
> *Oh, don't deceive me,*
> *Oh, never lea-ea-ve me —*

The tune is really happy: very high notes going up and up in a descant. I liked the song so much that I sang a little. But I sang *very* quietly, so as not to ruin the sound: the others all had pretty voices.

> *Ho-ow could you treat a maiden so?*
> *Remember the vows that you ma-a-ade to your Ma-a-ry*
> *Remember the bower where you vowed to be true!*
> *O, don't deceive me,*
> *O, never leave me,*
> *How could you treat a poor maid so?*

By this time everyone was more awake. We sang more songs, and talked, and laughed — I sang out loud on the chorus of one. We always almost shouted it in a Scots accent:

> *Oh you'll tock the high road*
> *An' I'll tock the low road*
> *But I'll be in Scotland aFORE ye. . . .*

Then I said, "Let's sing a song and then, at the end of it, all throw confetti up into the air at exactly the same time."

"Yes, let's!" Clare said. "What about 'Auld Lang Syne' for the song?"

"Perfect," I said.

"And, while we sing it, we can wish that we'll always be friends," she said, a little shyly.

"Or at least think of each other whenever we sing that song," I said.

Jennifer said, "When grown-ups sing 'Auld Lang Syne' at the end of parties they always stand in a circle and hold hands. Shall we do that?"

"What about throwing the confetti?" I said.

"We could do that at the end of the NEXT song. At really grand parties, they sing 'Auld Lang Syne' and then the band plays 'God Save the Queen.'"

Everyone thought that was a good idea; and, I thought, I could just hum and think of "My Country 'Tis of Thee" while they sang their words.

So we all stood up and held hands and sang — even I sang:

Should old acquaintance be forgot
And never brought to mind?
Should OLD acquaintance be forgot and days of auld lang syne?

I don't know why, the words aren't sad, and the tune isn't sad, either; but the song has a sad feeling. I felt sad, anyway; it was as though I was myself, but also outside myself, watching four young girls hold hands and sing a song about time.

I don't know how the others felt — everyone was quiet while Clare shook confetti into our hands. Then Jennifer said, "Let's not throw it all at once. It will last longer if we do it one at a time. Let's pause at the end of each line, and each time, one of us will throw hers, starting with you, Libby!"

I liked that idea and so did everyone else. They sang "God Save the Queen" loudly, and we all threw our confetti REALLY high. It landed on people's pajamas, and in their hair, and all over the blanket and floor.

Some landed in the butter (which we hadn't used at all, I noticed), too.

That was the end of the party. Jennifer and Veryan carried the blanket to the window and shook it, and Clare and I picked confetti off the floor and threw most of it in the wastebasket (I kept the box and some of the pieces, too).

"What on Earth are we going to do with all this butter?" Jennifer said. "We can't just throw it in the wastebasket: she'll see it!"

"Rinse it down the drain," I said.

"What DO you mean?"

"Dissolve it: I'll show you," I said. I took the butter, unwrapped it, and turned on the water.

I thought it would just melt like ice and go down the drain, but it didn't. I tried squishing it and pushing it down the drain with my hands; but all that happened was that my hands got greasy.

I reported all this back to the others and everyone was giggling and making silly suggestions when suddenly, the door opened, the light flashed on, and Matron stood in the doorway.

She was wearing a dressing gown, and her hair was in two long gray braids: tight ones, not one graceful loose one like Marza's.

"What are you doing out of bed — and at the basin — at this hour, Libby?" she said.

I turned around, keeping the basin hidden behind me.

"I was rinsing something," I said.

Sometimes, when we were getting ready for bed, we *did* wash our handkerchiefs in the basin.

"At one o'clock in the morning? I never heard of anything so silly. Get back into bed at once!"

I was afraid that if I moved out of the way she'd see the butter, but she switched off the light immediately and said that if there was any more talking or "silliness," we'd have to stand in corners again. (This was the latest punishment for talking after Lights Out: The whole dormitory had to go downstairs, no matter how late it was or how cold, and stand in the corners of the room just outside the Long Room.)

"It's odd that the singing didn't wake her, but the water did," Clare whispered when she'd left.

"And lucky," I said. "We got to have the whole Midnight Feast!"

In the morning, butter was still in the sink; some might have gone down the drain, but not much.

In the end we scraped it all off and threw it out the window. Our fingers, handkerchiefs, and the basin were all quite greasy by the time we went down to breakfast, but (we hoped) no one would be able to tell that the basin had been full of butter.

Chapter Thirty-three: Drawing In

The days were getting shorter and shorter — "drawing in," they called it. It was almost dark after lessons and completely dark by supper time. So in the afternoon we played in our study. In the evening, we had light lessons like Sewing or French Fairy Tales: in that, Mamzelle read fairy tales out loud to us in French, and I could understand them! (Of course, already knowing the stories helped.)

"Soon you'll be eating in the French Dining Room," she said — but she was teasing me, I think.

But the best part of these days drawing in was our study. It was a small room with almost no furniture — one table, and two wardrobes of cubbies. We used to climb on top of the wardrobes to play jacks — the carpet

The French Dining Room was a smaller room next to the main Dining Room. The oldest girls ate in there, with Mamzelle, and (supposedly) spoke only in French. I say "supposedly" because we were supposed to talk only in French during French Fairy Tales, too, and almost all of our conversations were in English, though we did speak it in a French accent and use French words when we knew them:

"Le petit chaperon rouge — aussi le petit idiot rouge, don't you think? Why on earth did she go into the cottage??"

(coconut matting) was too rough to play on, because the ball didn't bounce properly and it was hard to pick up the jacks from it. In America, I didn't know how to play — I used to spin the jacks, but that's all. But in England I learned how to really play. It's a fun game. We also played cat's cradle and made things out of wool (Clare was especially good at that); we had little rectangles of cardboard that we wove on, and empty spools of thread with nails on the top that we knitted things with.

And of course we talked a lot. That was one of the most fun things about Sibton Park — how much everyone talked and that there was always someone to talk to. And we read (to ourselves, never out loud). We read books, and

Jacks is fun, but hard. You sit down (of course) and throw the jacks on the floor. Then you throw the ball up, pick up jacks before the ball bounces more than once, and catch the ball—all with the same hand. You pick the jacks up one by one (one-sies), two by two (twosies), and three by three, etc. When you make a mistake—don't get all the ones you should get in time, or touch one you're not picking up, or miss the ball—your turn is over. Whoever finishes tensies first gets to pick the next game. I never got up to tensies, but Clare and lots of other people did, so I SAW the other jack games, like double bouncy (easier), flying dutchman (really hard). I liked jacks even though I wasn't very good at it.

In America, I knew cat's cradle up to this one— but in England, I learned lots more moves. The hardest one was called tramlines: two straight lines that you hooked with your little fingers. Cat's cradle was really fun; it was so satisfying when you learned how to do it well enough so that it could just keep going and going!

some people had comic books that told stories. There was one called "Angela Airhostess" about a beautiful stewardess and her adventures, though I didn't like what it said about America: "In New York she fell in with a fast, Scotch-drinking crowd." The Americans all wore hideous blue-green suits and talked roughly.

Those times in our study were cozy. Only our class was allowed in without permission — even teachers and Matron had to knock on the door and ask. We usually didn't let anyone else in: It was a place just for us. I liked it a lot.

Even though there was no fireplace or heat, it was never cold (probably because there were fourteen of us, and also because we usually sort of cuddled when we were just sitting around). One of the cubby cupboards went almost up to the ceiling; we climbed on top of it by standing on the table and then sort of pulling and scrambling up. When we sat on that, our heads touched the ceiling unless we slumped a little.

The other cubby cupboard stood under the window; when you pressed your face against the pane, all you could see was black, even though the Tudor Garden was right outside. You couldn't see any of the paths or even the sundial. Sometimes, instead of talking, I sat on top of it and wrote stories, and as Hobby Day got closer, I sat there every day and worked on "The Richardsons."

Finally, it was finished: thirty-two pages — on big, almost American-sized paper, not composition book pages. I read the whole thing out loud. Some people just sat and listened; some people went on with jacks and cat's cradle; but everyone listened, no one seemed bored, and several people commented on how long it was.

"Thirty-two pages! I expect you really WILL be a writer when you grow up."

I hoped that meant they thought it was GOOD, and not just — long. But more than that, I hoped that when Marza saw it on Hobby Day, she would read it — and that when she read it, she'd think it was good.

A page from "The Richardsons," the thirty-two-page story I wrote.

Chapter Thirty-four:
Marza, a Great Lady

I was proud of my writing and I did show off about it a little, but in an English way.

Once, I was washing my hands in the cloakroom (they were blue all over with ink) and an older girl said, "Libby Koponen! Your hands! Whatever have you been doing?"

"Just writing," I said airily, in a very English way.

She thought that was funny and repeated it to everyone else: "'Just writing!' says Libby."

Everyone knew I wanted to be an author when I grew up, and some people read what I wrote and said it was good. I wrote some more stories about The Crazy Old Witch (I only let

Part of the story I read.

Clare read those; they were too childish and too American for the others). To the others, I read a story about an English girl who had been ill and never had many friends until she went to school and learned how to ride.

But "The Richardsons" was by far my longest and, I thought, my best story.

It told about all the things the family did in the forest during the war, including all the children's complaints and arguments, and ended with: "The Germans were out of that part of England and Mr. Richardson was home at last!"

After I read it out loud to everyone that day in the study, I copied it over neatly, in ink, in my best handwriting, and gave it to Miss Tomlinson for Hobby Day.

As we walked around the art room on Hobby Day, looking at the things everyone had made, I wondered, again, what Marza (who was about the only person in the school who hadn't read it) would think.

She didn't say anything when she saw the story, but when she left the Art Room, she took it with her.

The next day after prayers she said she wanted to see me in her office. Usually, only seniors were called in there, and even they weren't called in often. Everyone looked at me, wondering.

When I went in, she was at her desk, sitting up very straight. She motioned for me to stand right next to her, so I did. My story was on the desk in front of her. I was standing so close to her that I could see right into her eyes. I was a little scared — they looked so serious.

"I read your story," she said, "and it was a good story. However — you made one mistake."

My throat started to hurt the way it does when you're about to cry and trying hard not to. I'd been so proud of the story and I had wanted her to like it so much and she didn't — I'd said something terrible, wrong, I could tell by the way she was looking at me.

She drew herself up proudly, like a queen, and said, "The Germans *never* landed in England."

I started to cry — I didn't know why saying they had was so bad, but I understood that it was a terrible thing to have done.

"No foreign army has ever invaded us," she said. "They have often tried; they have never succeeded."

She talked more and said a poem about "this little world, this precious stone set in a silver sea" and "moat" and "this blessed plot, this earth, this realm, this England."

I tried to stop crying and listen properly but I couldn't. I'd wanted that story to be good so badly. She stopped talking and pulled me onto her lap.

I stopped crying. I sat up straight and pulled my handkerchief out of my sleeve (in England all children carry handkerchiefs tucked into the sleeve of their jumpers). Marza looked at it and I did, too: a crumpled ball, wet in some places, stiff yellow-green in others. Gently, she tucked it back into my sleeve.

"Most wet and uncomfy," she said.

She handed me a clean one and I blew my nose and dried my eyes and the rest of my face.

"There, that's better, isn't it?" Marza said. She smiled and gave me a little squeeze. "Off you go — and it IS a good story, you know."

When I walked back to my form room I felt proud of my writing again. "The Richardsons" *was* a good story. Marza liked it.

And I thought about the rest. It was odd — I never would have thought of Marza as cuddling anyone. She didn't make me feel embarrassed about crying, or the handkerchief — it must have looked disgusting to her, but she didn't make a face or a disgusted comment; she acted as though it — and my crying — were perfectly all right. That's what being truly polite means: thinking about how other people feel and acting in the way that will make them feel best.

Before that, I had admired Marza, but I had been a little bit afraid of her, too. From then on, I wasn't afraid of her anymore, maybe in awe of her — she was a true lady. And after that, whenever I heard or read the phrase "a great lady," I thought of her.

Chapter Thirty-five:
Riding on the Downs

It was almost spring again and we were riding on the downs. The "downs" are little hills with no trees, just grass open to the sky. They look like the hills you draw when you're little. We were racing to Miss Monkman, who was on top of a hill; she'd told us to stand still until she got there and that when she raised her arm we could start — and we could go as fast as we wanted to when we were going uphill; going down we had to walk or trot.

As soon as Frisky and I got to the bottom and the ground was flat, I squeezed with my legs to make him go faster and he bounded into a canter. The grass felt short and springy. My feet were in the stirrups, my heels pushed down, my ankles acted like springs every time he bounded forward — but the rest of me stayed still except for my hips, which sank down into the saddle and moved back and forth in rhythm with his canter. I'd finally learned to canter and I loved it. It's hard to describe what cantering feels like but I'll try.

Your legs grip the horse, your calves especially, and your hip-bones move one TWO three (and then a little pause while the horse is in the air for a second), one TWO three (the little flying pause again). Your legs don't move, your upper body doesn't move — just your hips. Your hands are kind of pressing into the rough mane; they don't move, either, but your elbows bend in rhythm, too.

When we got to the top of the hill, I squeezed the reins and gripped hard to make him slow down: it's a little scary going fast downhill — you feel off-balance, as though you might slip out of the saddle and slide right down the pony's neck. And anyway it was against the rules of the race.

So we walked down but when we got to the bottom he jumped into the canter as soon as I squeezed — and up the last hill we galloped. In a gallop your hips don't move: you stand up in the stirrups a little bit and you feel the pony stretch out and jump, stretch out and jump, faster and faster, over and over . . . the rhythm isn't smooth like the canter, and it's so fast. You feel almost like the pony's taking little jumps into the air, pushing and pulling and stretching himself with each foot, and the hooves on the ground are so loud. Frisky wanted to win as much as I did, I could feel it. We went faster and faster — it was almost hard to breathe. I just stood up in the stirrups and looked straight between his ears at Miss Monkman until we got there.

We were first.

"Well done, Libby!" she said, and I patted Frisky and felt proud.

I'd worked hard at my riding and, even though almost all the other girls were better at it than I was, I still felt proud that I'd learned how to do it.

And I loved it. Nothing is as much fun as riding your best on a good horse. That day the air was wet, with that muddy late-winter, almost-spring feeling, and I *was* riding my best. My body was doing everything I wanted it to do all by itself. Without my even thinking, it moved in perfect rhythm with Frisky.

Maybe, I thought, next term I'd learn to jump; and then I remembered that I wouldn't be there next term.

Chapter Thirty-six:
"God Save the Queen!"

It was the middle of March, the last day of term for the people going home by car, and — in England — muddy early spring. The daffodils were out and everything had that wet, coming-alive smell, the damp gray expectancy of early spring. Some people like real spring best and some people like fall best, but I like that: spring just before it really happens, when the sky is gray and everything else is damp, ready and waiting, just about to come alive.

The people going home by car were leaving after the play, and I was one of them. My parents were in the audience, and when the play was over, they'd drive me to London.

The play was a history of Sibton Park, and it started with Buffer as the man who built the house. There were scenes of the Middle Ages, and wars — people going off to fight the French, or coming home from beating them.

The first scene I really liked showed Azma Haydray, who was quite fat and did look rather like a man anyway, dressed up in a red soldiers' coat, a black three-cornered hat, riding britches, and black boots with spurs marching onto the stage with some other soldiers behind her.

They were carrying swords and the flags from the church, the

Nelson led the English navy in the days of cannons and sailing ships; he was one of England's heroes. The dormitories Nelson and Trafalgar (his last battle — even though he died in it, the English won) were named to honor him. Before battles they sprinkled the ship decks with sand so people wouldn't slip on the blood.

flags real English soldiers had carried into battle. In the same war Nelson said, "England expects every man to do his duty" and died doing his at Trafalgar, on the deck sprinkled with sand for the blood.

They marched off, beating the drums and singing very loudly while Miss Day played a march on the piano.

The next good scene was the bachelor shooting himself in the library the night before his wedding (this really happened in real life, too, and there was a rumor that Sibton was haunted by him). His brother found the body. The girl playing the bachelor wore checked trousers and a jacket with tails. Her short, curly hair was brushed straight up so she looked like a man.

There were scenes of people leaving to fight in World War I and World War II; I think Marza's husband and some of her brothers had died in those wars. Maybe that was why she felt so strongly about the Germans never landing in England: because people in her family had died so that wouldn't happen.

The last scene showed a classroom. A senior was a teacher, in a grown-up dress with her hair curling around her shoulders and glasses, and the smallest day girl in the school was sitting at a little desk in the school uniform. Then I saw why they'd let her be in the play: because she was so little, she made the senior look grown up. The senior talked about history.

"In the twentieth century two terrible World Wars have entirely changed the position of Britain, and she is no longer the richest and most powerful country in the world. But in the past . . ."

A white, gauzy curtain moved across the back of the stage, and people — all the characters in the play — slowly appeared behind it.

"Oh, look!" Felicity said. "We're going into the pahst!"

(That was her only line. But she did say it well — "pahst.")

The bachelor who had killed himself in the library shouted, "A school!" and then pulled out his gun and shot himself in the head, and his brother stepped forward and said, "By gad, there goes my brother. He's done it again!"

That was the end.

When the bows and clapping stopped, the piano started "God Save the Queen" and we all stood up.

As usual, I didn't sing, but Jennifer nudged me and whispered, "Come on, Libby! Sing!"

Clare sort of smiled and other people looked around at me and smiled, too — they all wanted me to sing; and it was the last time I'd ever be able to. As soon as the play was over, my parents would be taking me to London, and then to Europe, and then back to America.

It would be good to sing "God Save the Queen" with everyone. I hoped I wasn't betraying the Revolution, but I wanted to sing it with them once, before I left, so I did.

The tune is "My Country 'Tis of Thee," but because the words are different the music sounds different, too — slower, more stately, sadder.

> *God save our gracious Queen,*
> *Long live our noble Queen,*
> *God save the Queen.*
> *Send her victorious,*
> *Happy and glorious,*
> *Long to reign over us,*
> *God save the Queen!*

Everyone smiled at me hard and then, without talking (we weren't allowed to talk after church and plays and prayers until we'd left the room), we went outside. The rain had stopped and it was really sunny — so sunny that you had to blink and squint at first and there, standing right in the sunniest spot, were my parents.

They were holding hands, which none of the other parents were doing, and looking around at everything — my father eager, my mother a little shy. She was wearing her pink suit, and they seemed younger — more happy and excited — than the other parents.

I was watching them when Buffer came running up.

"Oh, Libby, I thought you'd gone. I want to say goodbye," she said — this was her last day, too. She hugged me; I looked up at her — my head only came a little above her stomach. She was staring into the distance, over my head, and her gray eyes looked sad: What was she thinking of? Leaving Sibton? Growing up?

I went over to Clare and Jennifer and some other juniors, who were standing all together in a little clump on the front drive. Jennifer was proudly and excitedly telling everyone that she'd gotten me to sing "God Save the Queen."

"Here she is!" someone said and they all looked at me.

I was the only one who was leaving; they were all coming back the next term. They were waiting for me to say something, but I can't talk when big things are happening and this was starting to feel like a big thing — I was leaving.

The gravel on the drive looked dazzlingly white.

"Well, then," Jennifer said. "Write to us, will you?"

I nodded, and they all said they would write back.

"We have your address in any case."

My parents and Marza were at the gate of the Tudor Garden. My father was waving, my mother was smiling as though she was glad to see me, Marza was waiting for me. I looked at Clare and she looked at me; she gave my hand a little pat and kind of smiled. I looked at her and then walked away quickly.

It was odd, I had wanted to go back to America so much, and now I was sad to be leaving; my throat ached with trying not to cry.

Marza and I looked at each other for a minute and then she said, "Good-bye, Libby. If you do not become a well-known writer I shall be very much surprised."

"Good-bye, Marza," I said.

Chapter Thirty-seven: Going Home

Not long after that my family and I left England for France on another boat. We stood on deck, looking

> . . . *on the French coast the light*
> *Gleams and is gone; the cliffs of England stand,*
> *Glimmering and vast . . .*
> — from "Dover Beach" by Matthew Arnold

back at England. Behind the white, wall-like cliffs that rose — "glimmering and vast," just as the poem said — straight up from the water, I could see the bright green of the downs, those grassy little hills I'd ridden on Frisky.

I looked at them, remembering that, and how hard riding had been at first. I'd been very bad at it: My first report said: "VF (for Very Fair). Far too stiff. MUST learn to relax." And I had — my last report said: "FG (for Fairly Good). Libby has finally learned to relax and has really improved." It had taken a long time, but I'd done it.

I'd gone to Sibton Park almost exactly a year ago. I thought about that first night, and Marza; the sack on my birthday, and Hazel Fogarty kicking her sheet up in the air. I remembered Matron and being ill with Clare, and snug afternoons in our study — pressing my face against the cold window, and then writing or chatting. But most of all I remembered those pale sunny summer mornings when Sibton Park was new and strange to me, and how hard I'd tried there, at everything.

"Today is April first," I said. "The first day of summer term at Sibton Park."

My mother looked down at me and said, in her gentlest voice, "Are you sorry your little nose isn't there, being counted with all the other little noses?"

I looked up, and even opened my mouth to answer, and then stopped. "Yes" wasn't right, but "no" wasn't true either. It was a strange feeling.

Finally, after two months of driving around Europe, we took another boat, a Norwegian one, back to America.

For most of the voyage, I read on the deck with a blanket over my legs and the wind blowing my hair and the pages, too, when I didn't hold them tightly.

Sometimes, I went to the very back of the ship and stared at the trail of white foam — like a wide, white, sparkling road getting wider and wider — that the ship left behind it. There was nothing around me but wind and sea and sky and sunlight and, sometimes, seagulls. I loved being alone with that sparkling, churning water and light, with nothing but water and space between me and America.

* * *

As soon as my mother unlocked the front door I ran into our house — the furniture was the same, the walls were the same colors, but it felt completely different.

I ran upstairs. The hall looked so short!

My father had warned us that everything would look smaller — places from the past always did, he said — but I wasn't expecting it to FEEL different.

Emmy and I ran up to Kenny's, where his mother was gardening. She hugged us and cried, and said, "I always knew you'd come back like this!" And when Peg and Pat and Kenny came home from school, they were as happy to see Emmy and me as we were to see them. We stayed up long after dinner, talking, in the Tampones' front yard — the summer night sounds were just as I'd remembered them: the little insects, the leaves swishing whenever there was a wind, and, later, a baseball game on TV or the radio. . . .

The sky was dark enough to show lots of white stars when Mrs. Tampone said it was bedtime, and when everyone said oh no, not yet, she smiled down at us and said, as though she was really glad, too:

"Libby and Emmy are home for good now. You'll see each other tomorrow."

And we did: We walked to school together just as usual, except that there was lots more to tell each other.

And just as usual, we separated as soon as we got to the Big Rock.

On the playground people from my class came running over, waving and shouting until almost everyone in the class was crowded around me — everyone but Henry.

I kept looking around for him, but he wasn't there.

All the girls talked at once, telling the news and commenting on my English clothes (I was wearing my Sibton Park white-and-blue-striped summer dress) and my English accent (I tried not to have one but I couldn't help it, it was just how I talked).

One of the boys said, looking a little puzzled, "All the girls have been going around telling the teacher: 'A tomboy's coming into the class.' But you seem like a girl now."

In the classroom, I looked again for Henry. Could he be absent?

The room was like the old one: big, with the same kind of desks and blackboards and bookshelves and windows. Even the pencil sharpener was in the same corner, at the edge of the windows!

And the teacher seemed nice. She said, "So you're the famous Libby! I've heard so much about you!" The way she said that, and smiled, made her seem very warm-hearted. All the grown-ups I'd seen so far seemed warm-hearted, in fact. Kenny's mother had cried and hugged us! "I'm Mrs. Sullivan."

She showed me which desk was mine and then we all put our right hands over our hearts and said the Pledge of Allegiance:

> *I pledge allegiance*
> *to the flag*

of the United States of America.
And to the Republic
for which it stands,
one nation,
under God,
indivisible,
with liberty and justice for all.

Of course, I remembered the words — all of them. And I believed in them even more than I had before. Then we sang:

My country 'tis of thee,
Sweet land of liberty,
of thee I sing.
Land where my fathers died,
Land of the pilgrims' pride,
From every mountain side:
Let freedom ring!

Freedom! It wasn't just a word in a song; I really *did* feel freer here, in America: freer to feel my feelings, freer to say what I was thinking.

Just as we were pulling out our chairs, I saw Henry standing in the doorway, and he saw me. We didn't say anything (out loud), but his whole face said how glad to see me he was. I really, really like Henry.

We did signal whenever he turned around in his seat, which he did quite a lot.

Mrs. Sullivan shook her head, just a little; but she didn't tell us not to. Still, I tried to listen to her properly—and after a while, I did.

She asked who had finished their "reports on transportation." Hardly anyone raised their hands, only Henry and a few girls, and Mrs. Sullivan said she'd collect them after lunch. So I could do one at lunch and recess! I didn't have to, but I wanted to. I wanted to do well, especially on my first day, especially at writing.

When it was time for recess Henry ran over, talking. "I saw you start to stand at attention when Miss Kelly came in. You had to do that in England when a teacher walked into the room, didn't you?" he said with a big smile. "And you have an English accent!"

"I know," I said. "It's odd. I'm not English, but—I don't feel all the way American anymore, either."

He nodded, and frowned down at the ground, thinking.

"Maybe you will when you've been back for a while."

"Maybe," I said, not really believing it.

But I was still glad I'd told him.

"I know!" he said. "We can have an Iroquois re-initiation ceremony!"

"Like when we became blood brothers! Remember?"

He just smiled: of course, he remembered.

"And this will be even better," he said. "Now I know what they did in the real ceremonies. I even have some real arrowheads."

"We could use them in the ceremony—before the oath!" I said. "But let's make up our own oath."

"I knew you'd say that."

We laughed – it wasn't that funny, we were just happy. We talked until he went out for recess. (Now that we were older, Henry said, we didn't line up: people just went—or stayed in.) He turned around at the door and I looked up from sharpening my pencil at exactly the same time.

"Remember that china barrel?" I said. "You were right. Not one thing in it was broken."

"That's good," Henry said; he knew what a relief that was, I could tell.

The wildflower breakfast set, not broken.

I got some paper — nice big American paper — from the pile, and decided to write about riding horses! I'd start with the Romans — they invented saddles with stirrups to use in their wars in England and other places. I could describe what it felt like to canter, too.

I looked down at the paper on my desk (bright white paper, blue lines) and then around the classroom. The tall windows that went almost up to the ceiling were the same as the ones in our old classroom, but I'd never liked how MUCH sky you could see (it was too blank). Now I did like that blank bright blue sky. It was filled with light and wide open to anything.

I felt like that, too, and bursting with energy. English or American, both or neither: I was back. I shook the hair out of my face (like a horse shaking its head before it stretches its neck!), stretched *my* neck, and started to write.

The End

$\mathcal{E}$pilogue

I never saw any of the kids again (I knew I wouldn't, that was partly why it was so hard to say good-bye); but later, I went back to Sibton Park and saw Marza.

Her hair was white, not gray; but other than that, she was the same. I thanked her as well as I could for what she and Sibton Park had shown me and taught me and meant to me, and she said (she was always so polite), "You make it all seem worthwhile."

I went into the Night Nursery, and our study, and the passage where we lined up for meals. The macs and Wellingtons looked just the same; and so did the floor, where all those feet over the years had worn down the bricks. But the walls were different:

Marza as she looked the last time I saw her. I didn't think to take a picture: the photograph is from the school newspaper.

they were covered with framed photographs, including one of the whole school my first term there.

It wasn't faded or blurry, the images were sharp and clear, the paper glossy white. Maybe it was the pose (everyone so straight), or the composition (exactly centered), or maybe just an old lens or paper or process that produced perfectly focused, fine-grained pictures, with glossy whites and gleaming blacks and grays. But obviously, the photograph was from the past, and as clearly focused as a view through a telescope.

We were in the Lower Garden, where we had stories in summer, wearing our striped summer dresses. We were in three rows: the littlest children cross-legged on the grass, the middle ones in chairs behind them, the biggest ones standing up behind them. Everyone sat, or stood, very straight, with her hands neatly folded in her lap, smiling politely — everyone except one child in the front row. That child was sprawled on the grass, chin up, staring into the camera, not exactly smiling, but not sad, either — confident, even defiant, ready for anything: "Go ahead — just try and make me do it." She looked as if she'd be glad to fight anyone who tried to make her do anything, but was pretty sure no one would try. I thought she looked spunky and very American. That was me, when I first went to Sibton Park, before I learned to think about other people and care what they thought about me.

Temper

"Blow out the light," they said, they said,
(She'd got to the very last page);
"Blow out the light," they said, they said,
"It's dreadfully wicked to read in bed!"
Her eyes grew black and her face got red
And she blew in a terrible rage.

She put out the moon, she did, she did,
So frightfully hard she blew,
She put out the moon, she did, she did . . .

— Rose Fyleman

To anyone
who has read this book:

Most grown-ups, especially my friends' mothers, liked me better after England, when I'd become politer; but it *was* fun to do the kinds of things my friends and I did before that happened. If you'd like to read more about them, go to my Web site, ifyoulovetoread.com. There are chapters that aren't in this book, color versions of the pictures that are, my favorite fairy tales, and letters from readers.

If you would like to make a comment about the book or tell me something about you, please write to me:

Libby@ifyoulovetoread.com

I'll write back — unless I become so famous that I get hundreds of letters a week. But I doubt that I'll ever be *that* famous, even if Marza turns out to be right about my becoming a "well-known writer."

Thank you for reading my book.

Your friend,
Libby Koponen